The Last Days of
POE

Airship 27 Productions

TM

The Last Days of
POE

R.A. Jones

CHAPTER 1

The night offers no protection, provides no cover from the evils that lurk all around us. Rather, it conceals them from our sight, allows them to sneak up upon us on cat feet until they are ready to pounce.

It was a clear, cool night, that evening of October 3, 1849 as Joseph Walker stepped through the door of Ryan's Tavern in Baltimore and out onto the sidewalk.

He stood there for a lazy minute, breathing in deeply of autumn air that was chilled enough to be refreshing but not cold enough to send burning fingers of sensation through the lungs. So pleasant was the evening that he decided to walk home rather than try to hail a carriage at this late hour.

Many times, over the duration of his life, Walker would wish that he had done otherwise.

At first, the only sound he heard was the soft shuffle of his own shoes; he had partaken of just enough spirits to make his gait slightly halting, his balance just precarious enough to make him drag his feet rather than lift them confidently.

But as he passed the yawning mouth of an alleyway, another sound intruded upon his senses. It was a moan, or a groan, like the sound a soft breeze makes while winding its way through the denuded limbs of a lonesome tree gone asleep for the winter.

"Hello?" Walker called out softly, upon seeing a shadow momentarily separate itself from one brick wall of the alley, only to then be swallowed anew by the darkness.

"Are you all right?"

The moans of the soul in suffering grew slightly louder. Unwisely, buoyed by the courage that sometimes come in a bottle, Walker decided to investigate.

Had he been totally clear-headed, he likely would have made no such choice. Much as he loved his hometown, Walker was fully cognizant of the fact that the level of violence in this city of Baltimore had as early as 1825 earned it the dubious sobriquet of *"Mobtown."*

So it was that even bravery fueled by alcohol began to wane as he strode cautiously into the maw of the alleyway. Each step led into greater darkness; each sound he now heard began to take on ominous undertones.

Each shadow or perceived shadow filled him with dread. Finally, seeing no one and fearing that he was being lured into robbery or worse, he turned to retreat.

And found himself face-to-face with madness.

"Aaah!" Walker wailed. The man standing nearly atop him was unshaven, his eyes wide and wild with insanity.

"*Reynolds!*" the wild man screeched.

Walker frantically pushed him aside and made to flee from the alley. But the madman gave pursuit, plucking at Walker's sleeve and clinging to him while continuing to scream the name "Reynolds" again and again.

As they reached the exit from the alley, the man from the shadows tripped, stumbled and fell heavily to the pavement. Freed from his clawing grasp, Walker started to run away.

Hearing no sound of continuing pursuit, though, he dared to cast a glance back over his shoulder. As he did, he began to slow, for the maniac who had accosted him was still lying on the sidewalk, unmoving.

In the moment, Walker chose to again act unwisely. He turned back and, with even more caution than when he had entered the alley he returned to the spot where the derelict lay face down.

Kneeling down beside the man, Walker took him by the shoulder and rolled him over onto his back. The derelict had fallen just within the circle of light cast down by a street lamp and thus Walker was now able to make out his features more clearly.

In a better time, the man's features might have been rather handsome, in an almost ethereal way. His thick, dark hair was disheveled. A small moustache rested amidst the lighter stumble of a few days' growth of stubble on his cheeks and chin, evidently having resided there even before the man stopped shaving the rest of his face. His coat and trousers appeared neither soiled nor stained but were of cheap cloth, slightly tattered.

His eyes were closed, but his lips moved slightly, issuing forth words too soft and garbled to be comprehensible.

All things considered, and given their proximity to the tavern, Walker's first assumption was that this poor fellow had gotten himself quit literally falling down drunk.

Yet, there was no evident smell of alcohol or other spirits about him.

Cautiously leaning down closer to inspect the semi-conscious derelict, Walker was suddenly and surprisingly aware that he recognized the man, having at an earlier time had occasion to attend a lecture and recital given by this very person who now lay rumpled and insensate at his feet. Walker could scarce believe his eyes.

Sprawled on the sidewalk was none other than the renowned poet *Edgar Allan Poe*!

CHAPTER 2

Richmond, Virginia: September 27, 1849.

The crowd on the loading platform of the train station had thinned out greatly as the conductor gave his final boarding call for the train that was due to depart at any minute.

"Are you sure you've packed everything you need, Edgar?" Elmira Shelton asked for the third time.

"Quite sure, dear," Edgar Poe replied patiently, smiling at the fussing of his fiancée.

She continued to fret over him, concerned within her own troubled mind that he did not look well.

Knowing this about her, Poe did not tell her that, at her insistence, he had paid a visit to their doctor friend John Carter that very morning. Following a brief examination and a few questions, Dr. Carter had suggested that Poe might be suffering from "tired blood," and recommended that he at least delay his planned journey for a few days.

Poe had demurred; he had already promised a Mrs. St. Cloud Leon that he would be arriving at her home in Philadelphia on a specific date, for the purpose of editing a book of poetry she had written.

"And as you well know, John," he had told the physician, "I am seldom in a position to turn down an opportunity for gainful employment."

Carter was indeed well aware that Poe often lived on debt and deferred payments; he had already assured the writer that there would be no charge for this brief consultation.

He also knew that Poe drew the attention and sometime favors of the ladies, and was rumored to have on more than one occasion returned those favors in one way or another. He wondered inwardly if it was poetry and shekels alone with which Edgar would be receiving payment from Mrs. Leon.

He smiled and winked at his reluctant patient. "Such things shouldn't weigh too heavily on your mind for long, though, eh, Edgar? The widow Shelton's late husband left her fairly well off financially, didn't he?"

"Are you suggesting I'm only marrying Elmira for her money?" Poe bristled. (Though he might not have been so testy was there not a part of him that wondered the same thing.)

"No, no, of course not," Dr. Carter assured him, helping him back into his coat.

"But I am saying that you should let your health and not your wallet dictate whether you make this trip."

"I appreciate your concern, John," Poe replied sincerely. "But I'm sure I'll be just fine."

The poet was now giving his worrisome fiancée the same assurances as he edged closer to the last car of the waiting train.

"Still, I wish you weren't going, Edgar," Elmira said, her voice trembling with emotion.

"I can hardly bear the thought of being apart from you for even a few days. Especially with our wedding day fast approaching."

"It's that very prospect that will lend wings to my feet and speed me back on my way to you," Poe told her.

Elmira stood with head bowed, fearing that to look at him would be to send her bursting into tears. But when he placed a finger 'neath her chin she willingly allowed him to lift her face so that his mouth could close down upon her own slightly quivering lips. She melted as always, moaning softly.

Yet even now, a nagging part of her suspected that she was not the only female upon whom Poe had such an effect. It had been said, truthfully she was sure, that women had been known to physically swoon at the very sound of his voice during some of his poetry recitals.

Elmira was of two minds in regard to her fiancée's effect upon the opposite sex. She was both jealous of that fact and proud that she of all women would soon be the only one allowed to call herself "Mrs." Edgar Poe.

Still, the thought that he, with all the moral frailties so common to his gender, would be spending days and possibly nights with another woman filled her with a trepidation that twisted her stomach painfully. Added to her genuine concerns for his health, this left her in a dreadful state.

"Farewell, dear," Poe said softly as he broke off the kiss. With a confident smile he turned and headed for the last car of the train that was already beginning to pull slowly away from the station. He stepped up onto its small rear platform, then turned to wave to Elmira.

Elmira returned the gesture, waving a lace handkerchief. But emotion then began to well up in her eyes and to stave off the tears that were bound to follow she hurriedly turned her back on the train and on Edgar.

The movement, however, swiveled her gaze upon a large window set in the wall of the station house and in it she could clearly see the vivid reflection of both the departing train and her husband-to-be.

She gasped loudly at the image that burned like a brand through her eyes and into her mind. Edgar was no longer standing alone on the rear platform of the train.

A tall figure now stood right beside him, dressed in tatters. The head atop its body was barely recognizable as human; most of the skin of its face was missing, exposing ivory white teeth and bones. Its skeletal hand rested lightly atop Edgar's shoulder.

In a frightening revelation, Elmira felt certain that this horrifying personage could be nothing less than *Death* itself!

Spinning so fiercely back around that she nearly fell, she moved toward the departing train. Once again, her eyes saw nothing but the sight of Edgar cheerfully waving good-bye, his mouth wide with mirth.

"*Nooo!*" the woman wailed, rushing forward as if in hope of intercepting the train, of making it stop, of dragging Edgar off it if she must and bringing him home where she could keep him safe.

"Come back!" she shouted, but the train was gaining speed and had pulled far enough away from her that Poe could not hear her voice, could not see the anguish writ large upon her face. At last he turned and stepped through the door into the train car.

Elmira staggered a few steps farther along before giving up in defeat. She buried her face in her kerchief, staining it with the tears expelled by her wracking sobs. Emotionally exhausted at last, she fell to her knees.

She would never see Poe again...alive.

CHAPTER 3

Men are, by nature, secretive creatures, often to their own detriment and that of others. That which is kept within often leads to tragedy without.

Edgar Poe had not told Elmira that he intended to make a brief stop in Baltimore before pressing on to Philadelphia the following day.

A small group of soldiers—some retired, others still on active duty—were gathered at one of the city's many taverns in a celebratory reunion of their graduating class from the military academy at West Point.

Poe was one of them; and though he had been expelled from the academy well short of graduation, many of his former fellow cadets had liked the young man and had eagerly invited their now famous classmate to join them in Baltimore. He had gladly accepted the invitation.

Strong drink had been a problem that had plagued Poe off and on through much of his adult life. It had become a bit troublesome again following the death of his wife Virginia two years earlier. That loss, combined with other personal and professional setbacks had led him to again seek comfort by crawling down the neck of a bottle on occasion.

On this particular night, however, Poe had shown what most military men would consider to be admirable restraint, drinking only enough to more fully enjoy the pleasant and revelrous company of his almost-comrades-in-arms. That was not to say he was exactly sober, of course; yet still in possession of most of his faculties.

As the hour grew late, though, the partygoers began to drift away from the tavern, singly and in pairs. As the time grew closer to the witching hour, only two members of the group remained in a corner of the establishment.

One was Poe, the other a slightly morose man by the name of Terrence Fuller.

"I should never have left the service, Edgar," Fuller said for not the first time. He wondered why his tongue felt so thick and ungainly within his mouth.

"But my father, my dear father, he never approved. 'A man in uniform never gets rich,' he said. 'Not unless he inherits wealth.'

"And he made damn sure to let me know I could not expect any such inheritance from him. Not if I remained in the Army.

"He finally wore me down, Edgar. I resigned my commission and came to work for father in the shipping business."

"It was the Army's loss," Poe commiserated. He was not nearly so inebriated as his companion was and, while far from stone sober, had enough of his wits about him to feel the man's pain and to sympathize with it.

"Do you really think so?" Fuller asked him plaintively.

"I'm sure of it. By now, you'd have been a full colonel." Poe raised his cup in salute. "Maybe a general!"

"You're a good man, Edgar," Fuller replied in an almost maudlin tone, patting his old friend on the arm.

"To good men!" Poe toasted enthusiastically.

"To good men!" Fuller raised his mug, frowning when he saw it was empty. "Another round for me and my friend!" he called out to a nearby serving girl, who smiled indulgently.

"And now I have the wealth my father spoke of," Fuller continued once a fresh mug had been set before him. "But all the joy it brought wouldn't fill this cup." He hiccuped softly. "Don't have my father any more, though."

"My condolences," Poe said sincerely.

"Have a wife, though."

"Well, that's something."

"Hunhm" Fuller scoffed. "She married the money, not the man. There's no love in my house. No children. No joy."

Poe did not know how to respond to this, so somewhat uncharacteristically, he said nothing.

"What about you, Edgar?" Fuller said, leaning closer. "Are you married?"

"I was," Poe replied, pausing to take a sip of his drink. "Her name was Virginia Clemm. She was my cousin…and all of thirteen years old when I took her to wife."

"Oh-ho!" Fuller said, weaving slightly even though he was seated. "I'll just bet that set some tongues to wagging, didn't it?"

Poe smiled wanly. "To say the least. So much so, that even I questioned my actions, my motives. And it's true that in part I was driven by my dread of living and dying alone."

"Men have married for far less noble reasons than that, my friend," Fuller said sympathetically. "And women almost always do!"

"You may be right," Poe replied. "But however self-serving my reasoning may have been initially, Virginia grew into such a beautiful woman both inside and out, proved to be so patient with me and kind to all, that I could not help in time falling deeply and truly in love with her.

"And now she's been gone these two, long years. Taken by consumption. Same as my mother and brother before her." He sighed deeply.

"She deserved better from life. She certainly deserved a better husband." Poe raised his cup, tilting his head back and draining its contents.

"I'm sure you're being too hard on yourself, Edgar," Fuller declared, likewise emptying his mug.

"Here, let me buy another round. We'll drink to—to—to something happy!"

"I thank you for the offer, Terry," Poe said, rising from the table whose legs were even more wobbly than his own, "but I think I'd best call it a night.

"I really *am* bound for Philadelphia, and the train won't wait for me come time for its departure in the morning."

"Aye," Fuller replied sadly. "Me, I think I'll stay here just a little while longer. Just a little while. It was good to see you, Edgar."

"And you, too, Terry. Good night."

"Good-bye."

Once outside the tavern, Poe stood on the sidewalk for a minute or two, simply sucking in lungs full of cool, bracing air. He was still sober enough to recognize the fact that he was not fully sober and to hope that the crisp oxygen would further clear his head.

He tilted it back on his shoulders and stared longingly and intently up into the starry night sky. He was fascinated by the cosmos and by what lay within, behind and beyond it.

Just a year earlier, he had pinned a book entitled *Eureka*, in which he speculated upon such things. In it, he had set forth theories on the explosive origin of the known universe, on its continuing expansion, on what would come to be called the evolution of man and on the possibility that there might be multiple universes all existing simultaneously.

Once again, as he stared awestruck at the sky, he wondered anew at the possibility that all this might have derived from some single, enormous cosmic event, some epic explosion of raw energy from which the very universe as we know it had been expelled

If so, was it beyond the pale to surmise that bits of cosmic matter might still be spreading outward from their central point of origin?

And was it not possible that this stellar event had likewise created other realties that coexist unseen or only vaguely glimpsed by our own?

Or was he simply mad for harboring such thoughts and ideas?

Only 500 copies of *Eureka* were published and of the few who did read it his revolutionary ponderings were mostly either ignored or ridiculed.

Yet he personally felt it represented his finest work, both as an author and as a thinker. And he wondered if, after it, there remained anything else worthwhile for him to write.

Poe's cosmological and professional reveries were abruptly intruded upon by the loud clopping sound of horses' steel-shod hooves on cobblestones.

A small, black coach, drawn by a pair of prancing ebony stallions, pulled to a halt beside the spot where he stood.

Seated atop the carriage in the driver's box was a tall, broad man who was similarly clad all in black, from his boots to the top of his coachman's hat. A black scarf, protection from the chill of the night, obscured most of his face.

"Are you Mr. Poe?" the driver asked, his voice low and slightly muffled.

"Mr. Edgar Poe?"

"I am," the writer replied.

"I've been sent for you, sir," the coachman declared. He held a slender whip in his left hand and used it now to motion toward the door of the carriage.

"Really?" Poe replied. He was puzzled by this assertion, unsure as to who might have summoned this conveyance for him, given that almost no one even knew he was here in Baltimore.

"It's literally a gift horse, Edgar," he muttered to himself, chuckling softly. A gift that, given his tipsy condition, he was inclined neither to question nor to decline.

"The Hotel St. Mark, my good man," he said formally, stiffening his posture—though he stumbled slightly attempting to step up into the coach.

The twin horses pulling the conveyance leaped forward at an expert flick of the driver's whip, throwing Poe roughly back into his seat.

The stallions quickly slowed their gait to a steady trot, though, and the coach began to take on a rather gentle rocking motion that served to quickly lull Poe into slumber.

It was a sleep without dreams.

CHAPTER 4

Poe awakened only when the coach came to such a sudden and jarring halt that he was nearly thrown forward out of his seat and into the floor.

Grumbling under his breath, Poe virtually spilled out of the coach and onto the sidewalk. He immediately began to fumble in the pockets of his brocade vest for the funds to pay for his fare.

"Yaaa!" the driver shouted before Poe could extract any money. He cracked his whip over the heads of his team and the horses leapt forward as if fired from a cannon.

"Wait!" Poe cried to no avail. The carriage must have been hurtling forward even faster than would seem possible, for it appeared to vanish entirely into the darkness of the night before Poe could draw a breath. Even the clopping of the horses' hooves had disappeared.

Poe scratched his head in puzzlement. He'd never encountered a coachman who didn't care to be paid for his services, and a little more besides if you please. He shrugged and sighed and turned away from the curb—only to find his befuddlement increased.

He had most decidedly *not* been deposited in front of the St. Mark Hotel. The building he saw looming up before him had more the look of a cathedral or palace than of a hostelry.

Somewhat Gothic in architecture, it towered darkly over him atop a series of wide steps. Arched windows stared but faintly out into the night and on either end of the edifice rose high towers. Stone gargoyles, their faces contorted as if in the throes of agony, were perched atop the building's cornices.

Even these distinctive features were viewed but dimly, for a heavy fog that had been absent when Poe left the tavern had now settled over the landscape.

Though it was an inanimate object, a mere construct of stone and mortar, Poe felt as if the massive building was exuding an air of foreboding.

Such did not seem to serve as a deterrent, though, for the author now became aware of dozens of other people coming from different directions, all happily ascending the steps and entering the building through multiple doorways.

None save he seemed to have come alone: they appeared mostly to be couples, though some moved in small groups. They had gone unnoticed by Poe before in large part because of the silence in which they walked; there were no sounds of gaiety or even casual conversation. Yet all were dressed as if on their way to a ball or gala of some sort: the men in fine suits, the women in gowns that bespoke of status in the upper classes.

Gazing at those who glided silently close past him, Poe saw that each of them wore a *mask* that mostly or completely covered their faces. This simply added to the disquieting atmosphere of the gothic palace, for each mask was molded into features that looked more demonic than human. He wondered if the faces they concealed were equally unnatural.

"Poe?" a gravelly voice said from behind him, causing him to start and spin around.

He was equally startled by the appearance of he who had spoken the writer's name. At first glance, he appeared to be a stunted, dwarfish little man. Like those entering the dark palace, though, he was dressed impeccably in garb appropriate for a wealthy patron's manservant, complete with formal white gloves.

Also like the others entering the edifice, the little man appeared to be sporting a mask, of a sort that enveloped his entire head. But while theirs, though somewhat disturbing, had borne a certain degree of elegance about them, his was hideously ugly and brutish, resembling the features of a bull-dog.

Yet upon closer examination, as Poe leaned down to more clearly communicate with the little man—he was horrified to realize that the creature was not wearing a mask at all!

Bristly fur grew from folds of wrinkled flesh. The dark eyes that seemed to glare hatefully at Poe were set deep within a receding forehead rather than staring out from the holes of a mask.

If some deranged and demented doctor, possessed of a twisted God complex, had somehow managed to transplant the head of a bulldog onto the body of a human child—this is how the product of his insanity might appear.

But such a thing was impossible…wasn't it?

"Speak up, man!" the pugnacious brute barked at him. Its nearly purple tongue—wider and longer than that of any human being—flicked out to snatch away a bit of foamy spittle from the corners of his broad mouth.

"Are you the Poe, or aren't you?"

Poe's immediate assumption was that he was caught up in a dream, for no other possible explanation for what he was experiencing leapt immediately to mind. Yet if that was so—how could he be aware that he was dreaming? The same for if he was somehow become delusional. He most certainly was not inebriated to the point of delirium.

Whether it be dream or delusion, though, he found that it did in a sense appeal to his decided proclivity to be drawn to all things outré and beyond explanation. Deciding in the moment to play along with this *danse macabre*, he bowed slightly in greeting to the little dog man who had so roughly addressed him.

"If you mean Edgar Poe the writer—then, yes, I am he."

"I wouldn't know," the dog man replied curtly. "I can't read. Wouldn't if I could. Reading is a waste of time."

"Alas," Poe replied, heaving a soft sigh, "far too many share your opinion."

"I am *Reynolds*," the squat canine said, motioning with one small hand toward the palatial building atop the steps. "You are to come with me."

Despite his earlier decision to give himself up to the moment, Poe hesitated. Dream or no dream, there were questions he wished to have answered.

"What is this place?" he inquired of his guide. "What's going on, and why was I brought here?"

Reynolds stood tapping a tiny foot impatiently before answering brusquely. "Your questions will all be answered—but only if you enter the house of my master."

"Oh?" Poe arched an eyebrow. "And who is your master?"

One corner of Reynold's mouth curled upward, revealing a long, yellow canine tooth. "Only if you enter," he repeated.

"The choice is yours, man. Enter or do not. I don't care which. There are plenty of others of your kind who have accepted the invitation."

Looking about right and left, Poe did now spy at least two other people who appeared to be like him; that is to say, not masked as were the others filing into the palace.

One was a woman. Appearing young and attractive, the gown she wore would have matched adequately those of the other women entering the edifice, save for a neckline that seemed to plunge scandalously low.

The other was a man of perhaps Poe's age or a little younger. He was dressed in a uniform of the United States Army. Poe couldn't be sure, due to darkness and distance, but the man's tunic seemed to bear the insignia of a captain.

The soldier and the young woman were not together but rather approached the entrances to the palace from slightly different directions. And it appeared that each was following the lead of little quasi-humans similar to Reynolds.

"Come, Poe—or go," Reynolds snapped impatiently. "But do it *now!*"

Poe turned away from the beckoning building for a moment, drawing a deep breath and gazing into the emptiness of the fog all about, then turned back.

"Lead on, my good man," he said formally, though his lips curled upward at the ends.

"Lead on."

CHAPTER 5

The tiny dog man Reynolds motioned for Poe to follow as he led the way up the steps to one of the entrances into the dark palace. Poe's head craned back, looking at walls that appeared older than this very land and that seemed so high above him as to touch the very mantle of the sky.

"Welcome," Reynolds said stiffly, holding the door open for Poe to precede him.

"Welcome to the *House of Lovely Pain.*" He cocked his blocky head to one side quizzically. "Or is it the *House of Painful Love*? I can never remember." He shrugged his hunched shoulders.

"Doesn't really matter, does it? Come in."

Passing through the doorway, Poe found himself inside an elegant though dimly lit foyer. A few of the masked revelers were congregated here and there, engaging in light conversations. So they were capable of speech, he thought.

Reynolds paid them no notice, leading Poe across the foyer. Their dual footfalls made musical, tinkling sounds as they stepped across a floor of finest marble.

Reaching the opposite side of the foyer, Reynolds halted a short distance away from yet another set of doors. Standing before them as if on guard duty was a tall, skinny fellow. His head was devoid of hair, his face gaunt almost unto death and his eyes were but tiny embers in dark, somber sockets. Yet he was dressed elegantly, in a blue satin suit.

"I bring a guest with me, Major Domo," Reynolds said with surprising respectfulness. The man he addressed fixed the pair with a hollow stare and sniffed disdainfully. He was clearly unimpressed.

"He is one of the...*invited*," Reynolds said pointedly.

Upon hearing this, the Major Domo's demeanor changed instantly and dramatically. He even graced them with a wide smile.

As he did so, Poe saw that several of the emaciated doorman's teeth were missing. Poe gasped with dismay as, from one of the gaps in the man's smile, a centipede came crawling out!

The wriggling creature slithered, seemingly unnoticed, down the Major Domo's chin and neck before disappearing beneath the stiff collar of the man's shirt.

"Once you pass through these doors," the Major Domo said, placing gloved hands on the knobs of both, "it will not be easy to go back." His beady eyes bore into Poe.

"Would you rather leave now—while you still can safely?"

Poe smiled. This was all so vivid, so real, that he was increasingly convinced that it was neither dream nor drunken delusion. Yet that very sense of it being a twisted form of reality actually made it *more* enticing and intriguing for him.

"There is no beauty without some strangeness," he said, lightly, motioning toward the doors with both hands.

Without further comment, the Major Domo pushed both doors inward and Reynolds ushered Poe through the portal. It was as if they had instantly passed from one world to another. From a place of dark and silence—to one of light, laughter and gaiety.

The writer found himself inside a ballroom of breathtaking dimensions and beauty. Ornate colonnades supported vaulted ceilings. Crystal chandeliers the circumference of large wagon wheels were suspended from those heights, both casting and reflecting candlelight in all directions.

At one end of the room, a small but full orchestra played a lively waltz while scores of masked couples danced and laughed and chattered. Others merely stood on the periphery of the dance floor, engaged in apparently lively conversations.

A cadre of waiters in formal attire wove their way in and out. Like Reynolds, they too appeared to be somewhat less than human, though their appearance was merely a disguise. Each wore a mask that resembled the head of a stork, complete with long and pointed beaks. They even walked in a manner meant to emulate that of the waterfowl.

Each carried a tray bearing platters of hors d'oeuvres and flutes of champagne, the balancing of which had to have been made all the more difficult by the jerky, strutting stride of their walk.

As one of the waiters drew near and proffered his tray, Poe reached for a glass of champagne. Then, thinking better of it, he withdrew his hand and shook his head slightly.

His canine companion Reynolds was neither so restrained nor delicate. With his tiny hands he still managed to shove three finger sandwiches into his mouth at one time, washing them down with loud gulps that drained a flute of wine. He belched indelicately before furiously licking his lips and jowls.

"Come with me," he then said, taking Poe by the arm and leading him along through the throng of masked revelers. A few of them called out greetings to Poe, though whether because they recognized him or simply because they were in a friendly frame of mind he could not say. One of them, a statuesque woman, took hold of his other arm and tugged him toward her.

"Won't you honor me with a dance?" she asked in a lilting voice, leaning forward and kissing Poe lightly on the lips.

The sculpted features of the mask covering the upper two-thirds of the woman's face were lovely enough to have been the countenance of Helen of Troy, and Poe smiled rakishly at her.

The smile froze when his gaze rose from her enticing décolletage to the eye slits in her mask—wherein he now saw nothing but two black, empty holes!

He swallowed back the acrid bile that rose in his throat and offered no resistance as Reynolds pulled him away from the grotesquerie in feminine form.

As they continued forward, he made serious effort to avoid eye contact with any of the other revelers.

On the opposite side of the ballroom, near the bandstand upon which played the orchestra, a wide staircase curved upward toward the second floor of the edifice. Reynolds immediately headed up the stairs, but Poe paused momentarily at their foot before following.

His attention had been drawn to the fluid motions of the man who was conducting the small orchestra. Tall and reed thin, he waved his baton with skilled ease.

As if sensing eyes upon him, the conductor turned his head to look at Poe, all the while continuing to wield the baton. Though homely and sallow faced, he graced Poe with a smile that appeared warm and genuine.

Just before he drew the baton across his own throat in a threatening, cutting motion.

CHAPTER 6

Poe paused for a moment when he reached the second floor landing, moving to the balustrade to look back down upon the ballroom below.

Like the waters of the Red Sea after the exodus of Moses and the Israelites, the throng below had quickly rushed back together to obliterate any sign of Poe having passed through their midst. The sounds of music, laughter and lively conversation were softer as they rose up to him but had not diminished.

"Come on," Reynolds urged, tugging at the hem of his coat. "You're late."

"Late for what?"

"The others are already there."

"What others? Where?"

"If you'll come on, you'll find out," Reynolds said brusquely. Poe, already annoyed by the brutish little…thing…thought that it would not take much more for that annoyance to become a genuine dislike.

Still, his curiosity outweighing his caution, he allowed the dog man to lead the way to yet another set of double doors. No servant was set to guard this portal and the two of them entered without delay.

They entered a room that was spacious, though no more than a fifth the

...he allowed the dog man to lead...

size of the grand ground floor ballroom. It appeared larger than it actually was, however, for it was devoid of any furnishing or decorations of any sort and lit only by a single, small candelabra suspended from its ceiling; its interior was no more bright than a typical dusk.

Clustered near the far side of the chamber were seven other people—five men and two women—who appeared to be as Poe; that is, unmasked and not dressed in party garb. Standing a short distance away from them were half a dozen and one fellows who seemed to be of the same sort of partly human, partly canine species as was Reynolds.

Upon drawing closer to them, Poe could see by their heads that these dog men seemed representative of several different breeds of dog: poodle, dachshund, mastiff, German shepherd, basset hound, terrier and greyhound.

Other than noting these differences, though, Poe paid them little mind. How quickly, he marveled, was the human brain capable of adjusting its patterns of thought to accept even the most jarring change of environment.

Not necessarily an admirable quality in terms of ones continued survival, he felt, for it could prove at cross purposes to the instinct to flee from the strange and unknown. But then again, it was quite likely that most others were not nearly so drawn to the unusual as was he.

"You will be met here by the master shortly," Reynolds told him. "You are not to leave this room until then."

"Why on earth would I want to leave such a warm and inviting domicile?" Poe said wryly.

Reynolds growled in response.

"Good evening, ladies and gentlemen," Poe said, ignoring the dog men as he approached the group of *real* people.

He was met by looks of suspicion, curiosity and indifference. He watched as Reynolds now left his side and moved to join the company of his fellow dog men as they quietly filed out of the chamber, then turned his attention back to the other fully humans.

"My name is Edgar Poe."

"Mr. Poe!" the younger of the two women exclaimed, separating herself from the others and gliding toward him.

As she drew closer, Poe realized that she was not quite so young as she had appeared when he had first spied her at a distance outside the palace: not so young as the image she sought to project. Powder had been applied heavily to her face in an apparent effort to conceal small wrinkles around the corners of her eyes and mouth. Her lips bore the appearance of crimson lacquer, while kohl deftly applied widened the look of her eyes.

Still, she was attractive in a rather tawdry sort of way, beneath the auburn hair piled high atop her head. Her dress was too garish and sequined to convey whatever sense of elegance she sought to project. Its neckline was cut far too low to be acceptable to most women of quality.

"We have a talented author in our midst," she declared, extending her right hand toward Poe. She giggled in an inappropriately girlish manner when he accepted it and then lowered his head to lightly kiss the tips of her fingers.

"Oh, my! How gallant!" she gushed, fluttering her eyelids in a manner clearly intended to be flirtatious.

Poe smiled, well aware of the effect he had upon some members of the fairer sex. For some reason, he did not look upon this as so much of a blessing in regard to women as he did when he was a much younger, daring and adventurous man. At least he tried to tell himself he didn't.

"My name is Candide," the woman told him. "Candide Swan." When Poe released her hand, she moved it up close to her lips.

"I am a *hostess* at a gentlemen's club in New York City," she offered.

"Hmmph!" the other woman practically snorted. Middle-aged and making no effort to hide it, she was the antithesis of Candide. Her pinched face was made to look even more severe by the fact that her mousy brown hair had been pulled back tightly and drawn into a bun. Her dress was modest, plain and sensible.

"I think we all know what *that* means!" she said in a scolding tone.

"I make no judgments," Poe assured Candide, then graced her with a conspiratorial wink. "I've always said that the best things in life—make you sweaty."

Candide giggled with delight, while the other woman scowled more deeply. She doubtless had no more use for the artistry Poe practiced than for that Candide did.

"And your name, madam?" Poe said, seeking to put her more at ease. He offered her a hand, which she pointedly declined to take.

"I am Mrs. Edna Benet."

"Ah. And, would that be of Boston, by any chance? I ask because I was born there and your accent speaks of it."

"I am," she replied. Her tone seemed to have softened little if any. "My husband and I had lived there quite contentedly until the time of his… passing. It was then that I moved to Baltimore to assume a position as housekeeper for a distant relative of mine."

"So you and I are not so different, dearie," Candide said in a mocking voice.

"We both earn our daily bread by serving the needs of men."

"How *dare* you?" Edna flared. Poe was glad to see that she was at least capable of indignation if not passion.

"Pay her no mind, my good woman," one of the men interjected. He, too, was of middle age; his thick, black hair was streaked here and there by silver. He had the bearing and wore the raiment of a clergyman, which was exactly what he was.

"It's obvious that you are a righteous woman," he said to Edna in a deep voice trained by years of delivering booming sermons from one form of pulpit or another.

"Thank you, sir," Edna replied.

"The Right Reverend Sojourn Farr of Philadelphia, at your service," he told her.

Candide looked at Poe and crinkled her nose is distaste. He responded with a smile.

"Enough of that," another man said testily. His pronounced, possibly deliberately exaggerated drawl clearly marked him as a Southerner. He was tall, his ivory colored suit setting off a face tanned by frequent exposure to the sun.

"My name is Justin Larou; I own a plantation just outside of Savannah, Georgia. And I was wondering." He looked back and forth between the others.

"Does anyone know why we are here?"

"You mean you don't know?" another man said. He was short and somewhat slight of build. Poe sensed that there was a sort of wiry strength about him, though, and his eyes constantly moved about as if he was suspicious of everyone and everything about him.

As indeed he was. In his native New England, Edward Carp had been a successful highwayman until heat from increasingly vigilant constables had convinced him of the desirability of moving to an even warmer but friendlier clime.

"I *thought* I was on my way to see a banker," yet another member of this disparate little band said in a gravely voice.

"What sort of bank business were you planning to conduct at this time of night?" Carp asked him. He smiled slightly, suspecting he may have just met a kindred if more covert spirit.

"The *private* kind, sir," the businessman replied indignantly. The oldest of this group, he bore a belly that bespoke of prosperity and the pale features of a man who seldom saw the light of day during his endeavors.

"In this town," he said smugly, "when George Porter wants a meeting—he is usually accommodated!"

Poe cringed inside. He made it a habit to dislike anyone who referred to himself in the third person.

"A fine corps we find ourselves amongst, eh?" the last member to speak said as he sidled close to Poe. He was a fine figure of a man, the writer thought, dressed simply but smartly in the uniform of the day of an Army officer. His blond hair was thick and wavy, his blue eyes flashed from a fresh and clean-shaven face.

"And how did *you* come to join the ranks of our merry band, Captain —?" Poe asked.

"Albert Montgomery, at your service, sir," the officer replied. "I am on leave, making my way from Washington City to visit family and friends in New York." His brow furrowed.

"To be honest, I'm not entirely sure how I came to be here instead."

"Mystery abounds, Captain," Poe replied, chuckling lightly.

All the members of the small entourage then began to speak almost simultaneously over each other in a babble of confusion that brought no illumination to their odd situation.

All such chatter stopped virtually in mid-syllable when almost all the lights were somehow extinguished as one. What had been a dimly lit room was now plunged into near darkness.

The verbal outpouring that followed seemed of equal parts fear, anger and confusion. It, too, was abruptly cut off by a loud wailing sound that then descended a few octaves and resolved itself into the notes of a large, unseen pipe organ. The music that issued from it was dark and ominous: a blend of fugue and dirge.

The next sound they heard was not musical but mechanical, as of large metal gears gnashing together like giant adamantine teeth.

To the accompaniment of this grating noise, a large circular section of the floor near one end of the chamber began to rise, its bulk visible even in the faint light. Poe's innate curiosity led him to step toward this and the others followed. When the circular section reached a height of about one foot above floor level, it stopped its ascent with a clanking of gears.

"What the devil is going on here?" Captain Montgomery snarled.

"Careful, Captain," Reverend Farr warned in a hushed voice. "Invoke the name of the Lord if you must, but not that of Lucifer."

"I doubt Old Scratch would require an invitation to put in an appearance," Poe quipped, eliciting a scathing glare from both Farr and Edna Benet.

A low, mechanized groan quieted them all as a trapdoor slid open it the middle of the raised platform. Through the opening rose a column of pale light, inside of which danced motes of dust.

With more clanking of gears, a heavily shadowed figure was elevated up through the trapdoor from somewhere below. The onlookers could see it had the general shape of a man, but no more.

Several of them gasped aloud as, with a popping sound a series of mirrored floor lamps, such as the stage lights used in the theatre, flared to life from all around the platform, casting their glow upon the shadowed figure and revealing it fully.

Upon seeing it, Poe reflected that the man standing before and slightly above them looked like he might have stepped out from some devilish medieval nightmare!

CHAPTER 7

The man who now seemed to tower over them was well over six feet tall and of large physical dimensions.

Atop his head, adding even further to his height sat a wide-brimmed red hat. The left side of the brim was turned up and pinned to its flat crown. Inside the fold thus created was nestled a large white plume.

A crimson doublet was worn over a black shirt with puffed sleeves tightly buttoned at the wrists. A red cravat held the blouse closed at the neck.

His red Venetian breeches were tucked into the tops of black knee-high boots that were made of soft calfskin. Short black gloves snugly covered fingers that were surprisingly long and delicate seeming for one so otherwise large in size.

Behind the man trailed a silken red cape tied by a cord that crossed over the top of his right shoulder and under his left arm. Around its edges, a narrow band of fine, white ermine fur richly trimmed the cape.

In his right hand he held a tall walking stick carved from glistening mahogany. Atop the staff sat a large, blood red sapphire.

The most disturbing aspect of this new arrival's appearance was the red mask he wore. Save for round openings through which peered intense black eyes, the mask covered his face entirely. Its features had been sculpted to resemble a bare human skull.

"Welcome, my friends, to the *Masque Diabolique*," the fearsome looking individual finally said, in a sepulchral voice that caused the fine hairs on the back of Poe's neck to rise.

"I am your host for this celebration of all things macabre. It is one whose roots and traditions go back for centuries." He looked upward and released a loud, almost theatrical sigh.

"I do so miss the Borgias."

"What does that even mean?" Captain Montgomery demanded. "Just who in blazes are you?"

"My true name matters not," the masked figure replied. Again belying his size, he nimbly hopped down from the raised platform and approached them in smooth strides. His eyes seemed fixed particularly upon Poe.

"But given that one member of your party inspired my current look—or did *I* inspire his imagination?—you may all call me—" He spread his arms dramatically.

"*Red Death!*"

"You can't be serious!" Reverend Farr gasped in revulsion.

"As serious as sin, Parson," Red Death said, leaning close to the clergyman and tapping him lightly on the chest with the jeweled tip of his walking stick.

Not waiting for any further response from the flushed, sputtering Farr, Red Death spun around, causing all to step back to avoid his flapping cloak.

"Follow me," he commanded and led the small group toward what appeared to be a bare wall of the chamber. As they approached, however, Poe could see it was actually a ceiling to floor curtain.

"This way," Red Death said, sweeping part of the curtain aside to form an opening through which they all passed.

They found themselves standing on a wide balcony that looked down on the main ballroom on the floor below.

The music still played and the dancing continued unabated, amidst much laughter and occasional shrieking. Along the outer fringe of the dance floor couple could be seen locked in passionate embraces that hinted at far more to come. The stork-like waiters worked diligently to keep the liquor flowing like a river.

"Look at them," Red Death said admiringly. "Such joy, such excitement."

"Such debauchery, you mean!" Reverend Farr snapped. "We saw it all on our way in. It's like some obscene bacchanal from the depths of Sodom and Gomorrah!"

"Looks like *fun!*" Candide Swan exclaimed, clapping her hands and giggling.

"Hussy!" Edna Benet sniffed.

"Dried up old prune!" Candide rejoined.

"My wonderful *Masque Diabolique* is held but once a year," Red Death explained, wisely ignoring the catty exchange between the two women.

"Always at a different time, always in a different location…and always by invitation only."

"I received no such invitation!" Edna declaimed.

"Of course you did, madam," Red Death replied breezily. "You all did. They simply weren't *written* invitations!"

Turning away from the balcony's railing, Red Death made a sweeping motion of his arm that seemed to encompass all the members of this group he had assembled.

"In fact, the eight of you are this year's most *special* guests at the *Masque!*"

"How is that possible, sir?" Justin Larou pressed. "I don't even know any of these people—any more than I know *you!*"

"I trust that will be rectified in due time, Monsieur Larou," Red Death replied. Poe mentally noted that their mysterious host somehow seemed to be already quite familiar with all of them.

"First, though," the masked man continued, "*dinner* awaits!"

Again taking the lead, he brushed past them off the balcony, once more through the curtain, then to the opposite side of the chamber before escorting them through yet another set of double doors.

The group now found itself in a small, brightly-lit banquet hall. At its center stood a long table upon which blazed small candelabra. Neatly dressed servants—again, men in stork masks—moved briskly back and forth preparing the individual place settings.

"Excuse me, Mister…uh, Death," George Porter said.

"Yes?"

"It seems to me, from what I have observed and what I suspect remains to be seen—that this estate of yours is far larger in size and scope even than it appeared to be from the outside."

"Yes," Red Death concurred. "Isn't that amazing?" He strolled over to one end of the banquet table, to stand beside a chair that rose slightly higher than the others arranged around it.

"As host, I will presume to seat myself at the head of the table," he said. "Mr. Poe—would you take the seat at my right?"

"If that is your wish."

"Oh, it is, it is!" With both hands, Red Death made a downward motion.

"The rest of you, feel free to sit wherever you like. Please!" He chuckled lightly, making a noise that to Poe sounded like that of a phlegm-plagued asthmatic.

From somewhere, more waiters brought platters of food and carafes of wine. These servants represented all manner of creatures in the design of the masks they wore: from the mundane—a cat—to the exotic—a zebra.

"Please, don't stand—or sit—on ceremony," Red Death urged his reluctant guests. "Help yourselves to whatever looks appealing."

"I don't even know what half these dishes *are*," Captain Montgomery, accustomed to much simpler Army fare said, before taking a healthy gulp from his goblet, "but your wine, sir, is excellent!"

Actually, Poe thought as he partook of a measured sip from his own cup, the wine was not nearly so good as the soldier made it out to be. Judging by the way that the captain eagerly refilled his goblet from the nearest carafe, Poe suspected that the *quality* of the brew was not so important to Montgomery as was the *quantity*. Still, he was not one to judge, given his own history with the spirits.

"Extravagant, that's what it is," Edna Benet sniffed with undisguised disapproval. "This whole place reeks of it. Good money poured after bad."

"You're a penny pincher, are you, old girl?" Edward Carp jibed lightly.

"A penny saved is a penny earned, young man," Edna scolded back.

"Indeed it is, good lady," Red Death surprised her by agreeing. He then winked at Candide Swan, though.

"But who wants to be saved, eh?"

Candide rewarded him with a smile and a giggle.

"Your…staff is certainly well trained, sir," Justin Larou complimented as one of the animal-masked servants leaned over to set a small plate of fresh bread before him.

"They are *slaves*, I presume?"

"You *would* presume such a thing," Reverend Farr snorted. "By the inflection of your words and your own admission you are a Southerner. A prosperous one, by the look of you. A slave owner yourself, *I* presume."

"I am," Larou replied coolly.

"What a terrible thing to do to your fellow man," Edna Benet said with an affected shudder.

"My chattel aren't *men*," Larou sneered. "Any more than I suspect *these* beasts are."

"Well, *I* prefer property that is less troublesome and more easily transported," the outlaw Carp interjected. He was staring appraisingly at the solid silver fork he held in one hand.

"The utensils alone at this fine feast would fetch a healthy sum."

"Mr. Carp has an astute eye for such things," Red Death declared, leaning forward to rest his elbows on the table.

"He's a notorious highwayman, you know."

"Oh, my!" Candide exclaimed in feigned shock, though the look she gave Carp was one of undisguised admiration.

"Never proven in any court of law," Carp said with a conspiratorial smirk.

"Interesting," Poe said.

"Isn't he, though?" Candide purred.

"Not in the way you doubtless mean, my dear," Poe replied, smiling and reaching out to chuck her lightly under the chin with one finger, eliciting an inviting smile from the woman. He then turned his attention toward Red Death.

"If there exists a greater hodgepodge of individuals you might have assembled together, I can't imagine it," Poe commented.

"The only thing we seem to have in common—is that we are all your guests."

"It does seem that way, doesn't it?" Red Death concurred.

"But as you well know, sir—looks can be deceiving." He leaned sideways closer to Poe, clearly interested in the author even more than his other dinner companions.

"And what we see with the mind can be far different, far more discerning than what we witness with the eye.

"What of you, Mr. Poe? Of what frame of mind is it you find yourself when composing your literary works?"

"My wish," Poe replied after a few moments of reflection, "is to write as mysterious as a cat."

Red Death chuckled softly. "But the images you paint with your pen," he probed. "Why are they all so deliciously bizarre?"

"Because it is my belief that words have no power to impress the mind without the exquisite horror of their reality."

"But surely," Candide Swan unexpectedly interjected, displaying surprising insight for one of her admitted profession, "some would argue that such works could only spring from a mind that was deeply disturbed."

"And they would be right, dear girl," Poe replied, raising his glass to her.

"In my case," he explained, "I'm afraid I remained too much inside my own head—and ended up losing my mind.

"As a result, I became insane, with long intervals of horrible sanity." He stared rather sadly down into his cup.

"But I was never *really* insane...except upon occasions when my heart was touched."

He smiled wanly, gazing at Candide's silent, puzzled expression, and then lifted the cup to his lips.

"And is insanity then the wellspring from which your stories originate?" Red Death asked, genuinely curious.

"There is doubtless more to it than that," Poe replied thoughtfully. "I have often felt that a writer *looks* at the same things that everybody else does…but he *sees* something different. These alternate perspectives are the stuff of which stories are made.

"Yet there is more still. It is often said by others that a person who writes, or paints or composes music has a 'gift' or a 'talent.'

"I, on the other hand, have come to believe that what we actually possess—or what possesses us—is a *usually* mild and *usually* benign form of mental illness from which we draw our creativity.

"But it is not *always* either mild or benign. For from it can also come the *destructive* impulse. When directed against one's self, it can take the form of self-destructive behavior such as alcohol or drug abuse. Even suicide.

"And more than one artistic soul has descended into complete and utter madness, never to return."

"Yet you continue to embrace this potentially harmful artistic impulse," Red Death commented.

"I can do nothing less," Poe replied wistfully. "Nothing else. It is who and what I am. I write because I must. In the end, it is as simple as that."

"One should only write in service to the Lord," Sojourn Farr pontificated gruffly.

"Perhaps we all serve Him in our own way," Captain Montgomery offered before lifting his own goblet and draining it in one long, deep swallow.

"What delightful conversation we've had!" Red Death chortled, clapping his gloved hands together lightly. "And shall have again, I hope." Pushing back from the banquet table, he rose from his chair.

"But now," he said in almost breathless tones, "if you will again be so good as to follow me—I shall at last show you the *real* reason you are here!

CHAPTER 8

"I think I've had enough of this nonsense," George Porter groused, crumpling his napkin and flinging it down atop his barely touched plate of food.

"Time is money—and I've wasted all of it I intend to!"

"Be patient just a little longer, Mr. Porter," Red Death replied. "After all, it is the middle of the night; even *your* poor, driven employees are fast asleep." His eyes narrowed almost menacingly.

"I think you'll all want to see what comes next."

Porter glared at him angrily but as last pushed himself to his feet. He continued to complain sotto voce even as he fell into line behind the others as they trailed Red Death out of the banquet hall.

A relatively short but winding walk down a narrow hallway brought them to yet another unusual sight. Oddly, they had all seemingly become accustomed to such in this monument to the macabre.

Once again they had come to a pair of closed doors. These were large and constructed of thick oak, reinforced by steel bands. A heavy wooden beam held them closed from the outside. A not unusual portal in and of itself—but made bizarre by the nature of the two beings that guarded it.

They were serpentine creatures, but of a size and shape such as nothing Poe or any of the others had ever seen or imagined. Their scaled bodies were thicker than a robust man's leg, with most of their length coiled in circlets on the floor.

The remainders of their bodies rose up nearly five feet into the air and seemed to bob constantly back and forth in almost hypnotic fashion. Their eyes were red and threatening, their forked tongues flicked in and out of their mouths rapidly.

As had been seen on no serpent since the one that successfully tempted Eve with the dangerous gift of knowledge, these snake creatures had what could only be called vestigial arms sprouting from their trunks a short distance below the level of their narrow heads. Dwarfish but functional hands grew from their ends.

As Red Death, still leading the way, approached the barred portal, one of the serpentine guard's head lunged suddenly forward. Its opened mouth revealed deadly, possibly venomous fangs that snapped at the interloper.

In response, Red Death rapped the beast soundly atop its triangular head with his jeweled walking stick. The monstrosity hissed loudly, but snapped back into its place. Red Death looked back over his shoulder and shook his head.

"What can I say?" he complained. "Good help is so hard to find nowadays."

Now thoroughly cowed, and in response to a waving gesture of Red Death's free hand, the two serpents hastened to use their stumpy arms and tiny hands to raise the bar blocking the portal. After pushing the twin doors open, the guardians slithered meekly off to either side, allowing the humans free entry.

As soon as the members of the small group were well inside the next chamber, though, they heard the doors being slammed shut and barred behind them.

The room in which they now found themselves was immediately plunged into almost total darkness, save for one faint source of illumination.

Set in the floor at the center of the chamber could be seen a large, shimmering circle of pale light, surrounded by a stone wall no more than a foot in height.

"This way, if you please," Red Death directed them toward the circle. "There is no need to be afraid—yet."

As they slowly advanced toward the circle of light, they began to hear sounds seeming to issue up from within it. The noises appeared to come from multiple sources, yet blended into a cacophony of howls, shrieks and moans of despair and sorrow. It was an aria of hopelessness.

Nor were they the sort of sounds such as might issue forth from animals—but of human beings.

"Gaze within the circle—if you dare," Red Death challenged, stopping at the edge of the circle of light and motioning his eight reluctant guests forward.

There was a brief, understandable moment of hesitation. Poe glanced over at Captain Montgomery, who graced him with a shrug of resignation. Poe gave him a nod and the two stepped forward together. The others followed close behind.

Reaching the edge of the recess, Poe cautiously leaned over its lip and looked down. Below was what seemed to be a sunken pool, but one whose waters were swirling round and round furiously, bubbling and foaming.

He saw now that the illumination came only from the outer edges of the pool. The waters themselves were dark, almost black. Yet as he looked on, thin, oily tendrils as red as freshly spilled blood began to suffuse them.

Images lighter than the ebony waters then appeared just below the surface, as if someone or something was attempting to rise up out of its moist grip. The wails rising from the pool grew louder and more insistent.

Poe went down on one knee, bending over the low retaining wall to get a better look. Intent on seeing what appeared to lurk just below the bubbling froth, he lowered his face to within inches of the disturbed waters. Behind his mask, Red Death smiled.

"Aaah!" Poe screamed involuntarily as a human arm suddenly thrust its way out of the dark water!

CHAPTER 9

The bony hand attached to the desiccated arm flexed, apparently seeking to grab hold of Poe and pull him too into the pool!

Poe could clearly see the rotten flesh of its fingers before he hurled himself backward, tumbling awkwardly to the floor.

The other seven rushed to his side, with Justin Larou lending a hand to help him rise back to his feet. They all stared down into the pool with a growing sense of wonderment, fascination and mutual fear.

Before their very eyes, the shadowy shapes beneath the water began to take on more defined form. The figures of men, women and even children became evident—their bodies being caught up, entangled together and spun endlessly around in the churning waters of the circular pool.

It became evident that it was from these vaguely viewed unfortunates that the haunting wails and moans emanated. More and more now, other arms managed to thrust upward into the air. Unlike the aggressive movement that had sought to capture Poe, the hands in view now made gestures more reminiscent of paupers pleading for alms—or injured creatures begging for the release of death.

"God Almighty!" Reverend Farr hissed in revulsion.

"I don't know that I would call Him *that*," Red Death replied rather dismissively.

He exhaled a puff of warm breath onto the glistening ruby atop his walking stick before lightly polishing it with a satin kerchief.

"What…what is this thing?" Edna Benet asked fearfully.

"I don't know that it has an actual name," Red Death told her. "But over time I have taken to calling it the *Purgatory Pool*." He looked expectantly at Poe.

"Do you approve of my use of alliteration, Mr. Poe?" he asked rather eagerly. It was as if he fancied himself to be some sort of "artiste" and was soliciting the opinion or approval of a respected colleague.

Sensing this, Poe rewarded his mysterious host with a wan smile and a nod of his head, gestures that clearly thrilled Red Death.

"You mustn't take that name too literally, though," the masked figure continued. "What you see is not actually purgatory—nor even a portal that leads to that solemn realm.

"No. The pool…is something else." He paused, gazing down into the swirling maelstrom.

"Its teeming waters are populated by what could probably be best described as lost or wandering souls. Accursed spirits that for a host of reasons seem to have been unable or unwilling upon death to have moved on to their adjudged final destination: be that heaven, hell, limbo or the real purgatory.

"Some of the souls trapped within its waters are but newly arrived—while others have been held in its grip for what must to them feel like an eternity." He leaned over slightly, gazing down into the strange whirlpool.

"Who knows?" he then said airily. "If you look closely enough—you might even see the rightfully tortured spirit of *Cain* himself still floating about!"

"Is such a thing even *possible*?" Justin Larou queried in a hushed voice.

Poe replied, "The boundaries which divide Life and Death are at best shadowy and vague. Who shall say where one ends, and where the other begins?" He cast a wary eye at their host.

"On the other hand," he said flippantly, "you should believe nothing you hear, and only half that you see."

"Hear, hear!" Red Death responded, tapping his walking stick lightly upon the floor and giving Poe an approving nod.

"This whole thing reeks of *blasphemy*!" Sojourn Farr pronounced harshly. "Why are you showing us this foul display, sir?"

"I thought you might find it amusing, Reverend," Red Death said lightly. "Entertaining, enlightening—frightening!"

He then cackled, as might a wicked witch from some dark children's fairy tale, before making an inviting gesture.

"Won't you all step in nearer? Take a close look. You might find someone you recognize."

Though reluctant at first, all his guests followed the example of Poe and positioned themselves around the raised edge of the pool.

At first it was like gazing upon a large school of fish confined in a small inlet. Spectral figures could be discerned, but so entangled and swirling so rapidly as to make it nigh impossible to make out any but the vaguest of features.

"Looks more like a *soup* of souls!" Edward Carp quipped.

But then, as if it had been summoned forth by these eight living souls, one of the doomed spirits in the pool began to separate itself from the others, rising up slightly from the water's inky surface.

It projected the spectral image of a sickly, emaciated woman: one who appeared for all that to have died when she was but still only in her twenties. The specter issued forth a sound that mimicked that of weeping and held its translucent arms out toward Poe.

"*Virginia!*" Poe cried involuntarily, his voice catching in his throat and threatening to choke him.

For the ghostly image hovering before him was indeed that of his beloved child bride—dead now for two years!

CHAPTER 10

Acting on unbidden instinct, Poe lunged toward the spectral image of his deceased wife, reaching out with both hands as if meaning to pull her spirit free from the clutches of the unholy miasma swirling below.

Just as instinctively, Captain Montgomery grabbed hold of Poe and restrained him, lest his momentum plunge him over the edge and into the pool.

"I see you *do* still have it within you to look to the needs of others, Captain," Red Death commented cryptically. The Army officer recoiled slightly away from him.

"The good captain just saved your soul, Mr. Poe," Red Death then whispered in the author's ear. "If writers have one."

Poe could do nothing but stare back at him, uncomprehending.

Red Death raised his voice so all could hear. "If you were to tumble into the ethereal waters of the pool—you would become just as trapped as are these sorrowful souls!"

"Why do you taunt me so?" Poe asked in a pleasing voice.

"I prefer the word 'entice,'" Red Death replied smoothly. He next turned his attention to the group as a whole.

"Please—step closer to the pool," he urged. "Though not *too* close." He chuckled. "And see what you can see!"

As though compelled to accept the invitation, the others stepped in closer. All save Poe: having seen what horrors the whirlpool held, he now sank weakly to his knees.

The howling and wailing from the tangle of spirits swirling inside the pool grew ever louder, becoming a nearly unbearable, piercing wail.

As had the spirit of Poe's departed wife, one by one other spirits began to take on more defined form and rise up slightly from the swirl of souls. They presented more discernible images of both genders, the young and the not so young.

As the living souls gazed in both fear and wonder at the images thus revealed, Red Death strolled casually behind them, casting glimpses over their shoulders.

"Quite a list of tantalizing ingredients we have blended into our ghostly stew, wouldn't you say?" he asked at last.

"They were parents, children. Those who depended upon others and upon whom others depended. They appear strange to you, do they not? Yet also familiar to you." He waved a hand over the pool.

"They come from all walks of life. Each had his or her own unique story. But there is at least one thing that all these lost souls you recognized have in common." Red Death paused in his commentary, purely for dramatic effect.

"They all blame *you*—if not literally for their bodily deaths at least for their confinement to the pool below!"

At this accusatory statement, most of the onlookers burst into loud and vehement denial. Some, however—such as the thief Carp and the soldier Montgomery—clearly displayed at least momentary expressions of guilt upon their faces.

The same feeling swept over Edgar Poe, even though the actual cause of his wife's passing had been the insidious ravages of the hated consumption. Still, he thought—he knew—he could have done better by her.

Other women had often found him alluring, and he had enjoyed that feeling and the attention it brought him just as much as he reveled in the fame and notoriety with which his pen had rewarded him. He had even allowed his charms to lead him into more than one illicit affair during the time that he was married.

But while he had flourished, his poor, innocent Virginia had withered on the vine and died. In the darkest hours of the night and in his heart, he had wondered if his own actions and inactions had somehow served to speed along the degenerative process that ate away his wife's life.

"Why are you showing us this, you monster?" Edna Benet hissed, breaking an oppressive, uncomfortable silence.

Red Death's immediate reaction was to throw his head back and laugh. The harsh sound of his excited, almost giddy response washed over them like dirty water and echoed off the unyielding walls of the chamber.

"It wasn't *I* who consigned these tortured souls to the pool, madam!" he asserted. Edna shivered as he pressed closer to her. "Perhaps it was *you!*"

"Nonsense!" Reverend Farr insisted. "Pay him no mind, Mrs. Benet—he's clearly *mad!*"

This accusation did not elicit anger or indignation from Red Death but rather another round of chilling laughter.

"The whole *world* is mad, Reverend!" he cackled. "Hadn't you noticed?" His voice then took on a lower timbre.

"But as I am about to reveal—there is a method to this particular madness!"

CHAPTER 11

"The Right Reverend is not completely wrong in his assessment of me," Red Death now told them. He placed one booted foot up on the rim of the pool, gazing intently down into its pale light. As if this was a signal, the wailing and moaning sound issuing from the souls trapped within died down greatly.

"I and all the others who call this House of Pleasure 'home'—as well as those who merely walk its halls as attendees of our Grand Balls—revel in our love of all the hedonistic luxuries.

"But even a wonderful life filled with wine, women and song can in time become a bit repetitive and tiresome. Wouldn't you agree, Mr. Carp?" he asked, turning his gaze toward the fugitive highwayman.

"I'm sure I wouldn't know!" Carp stammered.

"Of course not. Whatever was I thinking?" Red Death lowered his foot and took a step away from the wildly swirling pool.

"Take my word for it; it's true. So, as a way to change the routine occasionally, while adding yet another sort of spice to our existence—we liven things up with a unique and special type of *game* we have devised."

"What sort of game are you talking about?" Poe asked.

"I've already piqued your curiosity, haven't I?" was Red Death's reply.

"As I suspect you knew it would."

"As I had *hoped* it would."

"Can we get on with this?" George Porter urged, impatiently checking the time on his large, expensive pocket watch.

"Were you always in this big a hurry with your *wife*, Mr. Porter?" Red Death replied mockingly.

The businessman's small eyes flared brightly for just an instant before

...gazing intently down into its pale light...

turning into cold embers.

"Where was I?" Red Death said flippantly. "Ah, yes. The game. You should be honored to know that the eight of you have been expressly chosen to be this year's *contestants*."

"What's the *prize* for winning this contest?" Edward Carp asked a bit too eagerly. Given the obvious wealth reflected by their surroundings, his avaricious mind was awhirl.

"Nothing *material*, I fear, Mr. Carp," Red Death said, seeing the immediate disappointment on the highwayman's face. "But one which *some* at least would consider to be far, far more valuable. It is a prize you have already seen." He extended his left arm and pointed down at the glowing pool.

"If you succeed in winning my little game—and it is possible for all to win or all to lose—the reward is *freedom*. Freedom for the trapped soul within the pool that has attached itself to you individually.

"That soul, or those souls, will be released from the inexorable grasp of the pool. It will be relieved forever of whatever misery has compelled it to remain trapped here—and be sent on to its final reward…whatever that may be."

"This is madness!" Justin Larou scoffed. "Do you expect us to believe *any* of this?"

"I expect nothing," Red Death replied. "Except a good competition. Whether or not you choose to believe in its tenets is your concern, not mine. But given all that you have already seen with your own eyes—is what I propose any *more* fantastical?"

"Games have *rules*," George Porter said gruffly before Larou could make any reply. "What are the specifics of this—game you are proposing?"

"It is simplicity itself, on the surface, at least," Red Death replied. "If you will only again follow me."

They all did just that as with a swish of his cloak he stepped away from the swirling pool of souls. All save Poe, who could not so easily tear himself away from its dark waters. He continued to stare down into its dank whorls, hoping for yet another glimpse of his Virginia: but such eluded him.

A gentle tug at his arm startled him from his reverie, and he turned to see Candide Swan had returned to his side.

"Come away, Mr. Poe," she said almost tenderly. "She's still there—and may be forever if we don't follow the instructions of our host."

"Quite right," Poe replied, squeezing the hand that had lingered on his arm. "Thank you, my dear."

Yet though turning away blocked the *sight* of the whirlpool, it did not put an end to the *sound*. The pitiable moans of those within tore at his sensitive heart like the talons of an eagle.

Red Death led the group out of this chamber and into a narrow corridor none had been able to see before due to the poor lighting. It was but a short walk until this hallway broke out into a large and wide other chamber. Set in its far wall were eight arched and open portals.

As they drew near to one of them, it could be seen that beyond its yawning mouth lay yet another corridor, stretching farther beyond than could be determined by the illumination at hand.

Given what apparent distance could be detected, Poe thought that George Porter had been correct in his earlier observation that this palace or mausoleum was indeed far larger in size than would have seemed possible from its outward appearance.

"You all entered my humble abode through one of its front doors," Red Death stated with false modesty.

"Your challenge now, should you choose to accept it, will be to walk the length of your respective corridors until you reach its eventual end, where you will find yet another doorway.

"Step out of the house through that rear door—and you've won."

"That's all there is to it?" Poe asked incredulously.

"That's all," Red Death replied. "As I said, it is possible that *all* of you might attain that goal; nothing would please me more. Also, unlike a foot race, you need not be the *first* to finish in order to win."

"Sounds far too simple to be on the up and up," Edward Carp said suspiciously, voicing the thoughts of all.

"Always looking for an angle, eh, Mr. Carp?" Red Death replied. "And you are absolutely *right*. There is, as they say, far more to this than meets the eye."

"Of course there is!" George Porter huffed.

"And now you're going to tell us what that is, yes?" Poe prompted.

"Ever the perceptive one, Mr. Poe," Red Death retorted.

"For one thing, as several of you have already noted, things such as space and distance are somewhat…distorted in this phantasmagoric little domicile of mine." He reached out and affectionately stroked one of the nearby walls. "Just one of the *many* reason why I do love it so." He sighed with contentment.

"The march from this spot to the rear of the palace is much, much longer than it would appear at first sight. It will require *days* of steady hiking to reach the exits."

"Still," Captain Montgomery said warily, "merely *walking* doesn't present much of a challenge. There's got to be more to this contest of yours than that."

"Ah, the military mind at work," Red Death said admiringly. "Why aren't you at least a *major*, Captain?"

Poe saw Montgomery flinch at these words. He bristled, but not in anger, Poe thought. More like...shame.

"And now we come to the crux of the matter," Red Death went on. "The *days* to come are not what will present you with your greatest challenges. It's the *nights*!" He chuckled in eager anticipation.

"The *sins* you committed against the tormented souls we just left may have occurred by day...but the worst, the most daunting challenges you will face in this little game I propose, this delightful distraction from sameness—those will come for you in the night. From out of the dark—and even from the not-so-dark."

"And what is the exact nature of these challenges of which you speak, sir?" George Porter demanded.

"I cannot tell you the source from whence the challenges will originate— but I *will* tell you that each will be crafted in such a way as to have unique significance to all of you individually. The people and things that will confront you are less than real—yet capable of rending you physically and spiritually." Red Death's voice took on an almost coquettish tone.

"To tell you more than that, Mr. Porter, might be *cheating*. And we mustn't make the game too *easy*. Where would be the fun in that?"

"Fun for *who*?" Edward Carp snapped.

"Why...for *me*, of course!" Red Death crowed. Poe could almost sense the man grinning beneath the cover of his skeletal mask.

"And for my brethren, too. *Wagers* are already being made on who will win and who will lose."

Now it was Poe's turn to pose a question. "You speak of losing, Red Death?"

"Yes, yes. In every competition, there must be losers."

"But there aren't always *consequences* to losing," Poe replied. "What of this game you are proposing? What will happen to us if we *lose*—if we fail to overcome its challenges?"

Red Death spread his arms, acting as if the answer was self-evident.

"What else, dear scribe? You'll *die*!"

CHAPTER 12

R ed Death's voice took on a deeper and more serious tone.
"The *lucky* losers will then find their souls joining those already consigned to the Purgatory Pool.

"The *unlucky* losers—will have their souls cast down into the pit wherein eternal fire awaits!"

"This is outrageous!" Reverend Farr bellowed, and every voice save Poe's joined him in indignant protest. After patiently listening to their outcry for several moments, Red Death motioned for their silence.

"Is it that you do not feel the tormented, trapped souls that are attached to you are *worth* risking your lives for?" he asked them.

"I don't think they'd want us to *die* for them!" Captain Montgomery asserted, perhaps sounding a little too defensive for a military man.

"Perhaps you're right," Red Death conceded, shrugging his wide shoulders.

"Of *course* he is," Edward Carp declared. Several of the others were quick to voice their agreement.

"And did any of *them* ask to die?" Poe said somberly, and the others again fell silent. "Are any of them in that horrible pool by *choice*?"

"Still," Justin Larou said. "It isn't *our* fault they ended up in there."

"Really?" Poe replied. "Our host indicated it is."

"And why should we trust the word of a masked man we don't even know?" George Porter blustered.

"An excellent point, sir," Poe said to him. "But why have we believed *anything* we have seen or heard tonight? Hasn't it all been utterly unbelievable?"

In their hearts, they all knew he was right. But *something* had led them all to this place: the same something that compelled them to believe what their physical senses had seen and heard, no matter how fantastical it appeared.

Perhaps they had been bewitched. Or perhaps man's primordial belief in the supernatural was so deeply ingrained in their collective psyche that they not only gave it credence but felt compelled to plumb its depths even at the risk of their sanity and their lives.

Their discussions ended abruptly when Red Death loudly rapped his walking stick against the floor to gain their attention.

"There's more that you should know," he told them.

"Of course there is," Edward Carp said cynically as Red Death continued.

"I must warn you that once this game officially begins—you will not be allowed to quit. To quit—is to die."

"This is *madness!*" Edna Benet exclaimed.

"However," Red Death said more loudly, "it is for that very reason that none of you will be *compelled* to compete. If you do not wish to participate—say so now and you are free to leave."

More than one of them heaved a sigh of relief.

"One thing you should know, though. This is a one time only opportunity you are being afforded. This will be the only chance the various souls you glimpsed in the pool will have for redemption.

"No matter how many times this game may be played in the future—those particular souls will never again be granted the opportunity to escape from their present state of torment. They will remain lost and trapped forever." Red Death paused to let his words fully sink in.

"The choice is yours."

"Madness!" Edna Benet repeated.

"It's worse than that, madam," Sojourn Farr said.

"You don't think any of this is *real*, do you?" Edward Carp sneered. "It's a trick, a hoax. Maybe even some kind of fraud meant to squeeze money out of us."

"Our host has made no such demand," Captain Montgomery reminded him.

"Not yet," Carp retorted. "You make sure the fish has firmly bitten down on the hook before you yank the line on him."

"I agree," Justin Larou weighed in.

"What about you, Mr. Poe?" Candide Swan asked, placing her hand on the writer's arm.

"If any one of us qualifies as being an expert in all things macabre, it's you. What do you think of all this?"

Poe patted her hand. "If we cannot comprehend God in His visible works—how then in his inconceivable *thoughts*, that call the works into being?" His words brought nothing but a look of puzzlement to Candide's face.

"What the hell does that mean?" snapped the plantation owner Larou. "What does any of this mean?"

"As always, mysteries force a man to think," Poe quipped, "and so injure his health."

"Are you calling me stupid, Yankee?" Larou replied, balling his fists and stepping toward Poe menacingly.

"Calm down, friend," Captain Montgomery said, interjecting his body between Larou and Poe.

"I'm pretty sure that whatever this competition is—it doesn't require us to literally fight each other."

"Blasphemy," Reverend Farr barked. "That's what this is: vile, despicable blasphemy!"

While seeming to take delight in their arguments, Red Death was also growing impatient with his guests and their ramblings.

"What is it to be, ladies and gentlemen? Will you participate in our little competition or not?"

"Certainly not!" "It's foolishness!" "Let me out of here!"

"I'll play your game."

The four words were spoken firmly by Edgar Poe and caused all the others to instantly fall silent as they saw him separate from the group and move over to where Red Death stood waiting.

"I was sure you would, Mr. Poe," their masked host said.

CHAPTER 13

"You *are* insane, man!" Reverend Farr bellowed, and several of the others nodded their heads in agreement.

One who did not was Candide Swan.

"Why not?" she said flippantly before sashaying over to join Poe in standing beside Red Death.

"What have I got to lose?"

"Your life—and your soul," Poe replied somberly.

"The former is nothing but currency," she said. "And the other..." She smiled wanly. "Well, some would argue that the other is already lost anyway."

"Every soul is precious to the Lord, girl—even one as stained as yours," Reverend Farr said in what he perceived as being sympathy.

"Does that mean yours is so spotless it's too good to risk for another's?" Candide threw back at him tauntingly.

Stung and shamed by this rebuke from a woman he considered to be of loose virtue, Farr's mouth moved up and down wordlessly. Scowling, he stepped forward to join her and Poe.

After this, one by one the others moved forward as well. All save one: the businessman, George Porter.

"Your fancy light shows and all the other gimmickry you've employed don't fool me for a minute, mister," Porter said coldly.

"I don't believe your sad story about lost souls."

"You think this has all been a charade?" Red Death asked, taking a few steps toward Porter. "A hoax?"

"I do indeed."

"Well." Red Death seemed to weigh these words. "But let me ask you this, friend. The soul—or illusion—that seemed to call out the loudest to you." He stepped even closer to the businessman.

"Was it not that of your *wife*?"

Porter stiffened at the words. "It was," he admitted at last.

"And you're so convinced of fakery that you don't wish to try to redeem her soul?"

"I do not, and with very good reason," Porter snapped. "There is no such thing as souls!" He ignored the startled gasp this brought from the lips of Reverend Farr.

"You sound very sure of that," Red Death said.

"Very sure," Porter replied. "The only things that are *real* are the things you can *touch*: property, goods, money."

"And what touches your *heart*, man?" Poe said softly.

"Only that which touches every other organ of my body, poet—my life's blood." If it was possible, Porter now held himself even more stiffly upright.

"Life is what matters," he said, "and the living of it. And when that life is gone—there is nothing else."

"Surely to God you don't believe that, Mr. Porter," Reverend Farr said in disbelief.

"But I do, Reverend," Porter replied. "My Rachel was a good wife—a hard worker. But her time to die came—and that's all there is to it."

"So, to be clear, you do not wish to participate in our amusement?" Red Death asked.

"I most certainly do *not*, sir," Porter blustered. "I am a man of business—and in business, time is money. I can't—I won't—waste such a precious commodity chasing after ghosts that don't even really exist!"

"And there is no changing your mind?"

"No, sir."

"Very well," Red Death said, sounding genuinely sad. "My servant will show you out."

Porter gave a slight start as, as if from nowhere, a small figure suddenly appeared beside him; having seemingly appeared out of thin air. It was one of the strange dog men—this one with the head of a mastiff. It had been this same creature that had initially ushered Porter into the palace.

"Good-bye, Mr. Porter," Red Death said. "And good luck to you."

Porter almost sneered. "It's these other, poor, deluded souls you've lured in with your false promises who need luck—not I."

"Perhaps you're right, Mr. Porter," Red Death replied, turning his back to the man.

Poe and the others watched in silence as the dog man led Porter out of the chamber.

"Last chance," Red Death then again told them, turning to face them. "If anyone else wishes to leave, you must speak up now.

"As I told you before, once the game begins—none will be allowed to leave until it is finished."

He then waited expectantly. Uneasiness, nervousness, even fear was evident in the features of those who gazed back at him. But none asked to leave.

"Excellent!" Red Death exclaimed jubilantly. "I'm delighted to see such spunk, such sense of adventure and willingness to face a challenge.

"But for now, I'm sure you must all be quite tired. You will be escorted to your individual bedchambers. I suggest you get as much sleep as possible. You'll need all the energy you can muster when the game begins bright and early tomorrow!"

As had happened with George Porter, the seven remaining contestants now found their respective dog men standing beside them.

"Hello, Reynolds," Poe said, hoping to sound cheerful. The surly little dog man simply growled in response.

As the men and women were escorted from the chamber, Red Death watched them without comment, his thoughts known only to himself.

Then he cocked his head slightly to one side. As he had suspected, even from this distance he could faintly hear the music still floating up from the lower level ballroom. It reminded him that the revelry there was continuing—and doubtless would for hours yet to come.

Holding his walking stick steady and upright against the floor directly in front of him, he twirled lightly in a circle around it before kicking it near the bottom and causing it to flip up into the air.

He nimbly plucked it out of mid-flight and spun it a few times like a baton before rapping it loudly against the floor.

Chuckling softly, he set out toward the sound of the music—meaning to enjoy a dance or two himself before calling it an evening.

CHAPTER 14

George Porter's canine escort left him alone as soon as he stepped through one of the front doors leading back out of the edifice. Relieved to be shed of the place, the businessman pushed his somewhat portly body to carry him down its wide steps as quickly as his spindly legs could manage.

Upon reaching the sidewalk below, he did take a moment to turn and look back. The fog from earlier had grown even thicker and heavier, though Porter thought it odd that it could possibly have grown so dense as to completely obscure his view of the manse.

It was as if the edifice had vanished altogether.

Still, happy as he was to be free of its oppressive walls, he gave the matter little consideration. Pulling the collar of his coat up to ward off the chill in the autumn air, he set off walking in hope of soon spying a cab he could hail.

A thought popped into his head that perhaps he should make an effort to contact the authorities and tell them about this madhouse and the activities being carried on within it. After all, that "Red Death" lunatic had literally threatened *death* to those who unsuccessfully engaged in his demented competition.

But he quickly discarded such thought. What passed for law enforcement in the city of Baltimore was at best spotty in the performance of its duty. There would doubtless be no one at all at City Hall this time of night.

And those who had foolishly remained behind when he had chosen to leave had done so willingly. Whatever happened next was upon them.

Besides, he didn't want to waste any more time away from work than he had already squandered through no fault of his own.

Porter continued on his way, intent on getting a good night's sleep and being back in his office bright and early the next day, with no regrets regarding his decision not to participate in Red Death's little "game."

He was sure Rachel would have approved of the choice he had made.

"George."

The unseen voice that seemed to whisper his name in his ear was soft and feathery—yet somehow chilling as well. He paused for a moment, listening, then moved on.

"George."

The voice speaking his name now sounded slightly more urgent. Spinning around, he peered into the fog. Some distance behind him, he thought he vaguely saw the shrouded figure of a person standing in the mist.

Fearing this might be a thief in the night—or worse yet, someone sent to try to drag him back into that madhouse from which he had just escaped—Porter quickened his pace in the opposite direction.

Having grown soft from sedentary years spent in a plush office chair and from culinary overindulgence, Porter soon had to pause to catch his breath. He bent over, hands on knees, the bellowing of air in and out of his lungs the only sound he could hear.

He fearfully cast a look back the way he had come—and now saw no one. He breathed a deep sigh of relief.

"George."

Though he still saw no one, he was convinced he was being followed. He turned and again hastened forward.

His eyes cast about frantically, hoping to spy a carriage or public house of some sort where he could seek refuge. Yet he saw nothing but the damnably impenetrable fog and the sidewalk upon which his feet frantically fell. He couldn't even tell what part of the city he was in.

Porter abruptly halted as he at length spied another figure in the fog: this one standing a short distance ahead of him. Prompted by what he increasingly feared stalked behind him, he felt he had no choice but to keep moving forward. His pounding heartbeat seemed to match the rapid tapping of his footsteps.

As he tentatively grew closer and closer, the figure awaiting him grew clearer—until at last he was able to see that it was a *woman*. His fear immediately began to subside.

She was very young, very attractive. Her body, tightly clothed in a chiffon gown, was lithe and sinewy, ripe and full. Her dark hair was not drawn up but allowed to spill over her shoulders. Full lips turned up slightly in a welcoming smile.

"Hello, George," she said in a familiar voice.

In the instant, Porter realized everything about this alluring vision was familiar to him, though only as a memory.

It was his wife, Rachel.

His dead wife.

Yet, here she stood clearly before him, looking exactly as she had when Porter first met her, more than forty years agone.

"Are...are you a *ghost*?" he asked fearfully.

"Until a short time ago," she replied in that same familiar voice that had whispered his name earlier, "I was *less* than a ghost, trapped inside that horrid pool. Surrounded, smothered by the dregs of society.

"But *you* released me, George."

"How did I do that?" he asked, genuinely puzzled.

"By bravely standing up to that twisted devil, Red Death, that's how," she replied. "By refusing to play his insipid game."

"Yes. I did, didn't I?" he said rather proudly, trying to make it sound as if he had known all along that this would be the outcome of his actions.

"So," he then said hesitantly, clearing his throat, "I suppose this means you'll be moving on to your just reward now, doesn't it?"

"Only if I want to," Rachel said, starting to glide sensuously toward him. "I am completely free now—even free to stay here in the land of the living." She reached out and he felt the light touch of her fingertips on his chest.

"That is…if you *want* me to stay, George."

What man *wouldn't* want this woman? Porter thought. She was young, beautiful and desirable. For a flickering moment, it occurred to him that he had no true, clear memory of Rachel being this attractive, this alluring— though surely she must have been when they married as youths.

But for young George Porter the passions of the flesh had soon been supplanted by the passion to succeed, to acquire material wealth. To achieve those ends, he had driven his wife to work as hard as himself—even harder than his eventual employees. To him, this made perfect sense.

After all—Rachel worked for free.

Porter had turned a deaf ear to her desires for motherhood and a blind eye to the ravages of time and labor, as she grew old and frail before her time.

On the last occasion when he had bothered to speak with his relatives, they had warned George that he was going to work the poor woman to death.

And maybe he had, he thought. But he'd pushed himself as hard and now he was reaping the rewards. Perhaps Rachel would have, too, if only she had been stronger.

But this young and vibrant Rachel now somehow miraculously standing before him looked more than strong and healthy. When he smiled at her she stepped closer and entwined her arms around his neck.

Her lips met his and they were warm and yielding, her tongue probing wetly. For the first time in many years, George Porter found himself feeling passion for something other than the acquisition of wealth.

Then came the *pain*.

Porter felt a sharp contraction deep within his chest, as if an invisible hand had reached inside and given his heart a vicious squeeze.

This was followed immediately by an electrifying bolt of energy coursing through his brain.

He instinctively attempted to pull away from Rachel but the effort simply caused her arms to embrace him more tightly, threatening to cut off his breathing.

His eyes grew wide and he saw that hers were also open—but they had no pupils. They looked like small black pearls through which swirled tiny flashes of light.

Porter gripped the succubus's arms, frantically attempting to pry loose their grip. When this failed, he began to flay at her with his fists, but found the blows lacked strength and grew increasingly weaker.

He could literally feel the life draining away from him. It was as if every year that his wife had lived was now being added to his own age in a matter of seconds.

His skin grew thin and wrinkled. White hair fell out in large clumps. His vision grew dimmer. His insides liquefied and oozed from his eyes and ears.

By the time the ghostly Rachel released his lifeless body and let it drop to the pavement, it was as shriveled and decayed as if it had been six months under the soil.

The spectral image of Rachel stood staring down at his corpse for several minutes. She then threw her head back and laughed maniacally, almost appearing to be a wild beast howling at the fog-obscured moon.

Like a dervish she spun around and around until her form dissipated and vanished smoke-like.

Back inside the palace of Red Death, within the swirling Purgatory Pool, this ghost projection returned to the source that had manifested and dispatched it: the true, trapped soul of Rachel Porter.

And for a moment, above the insistent wailing and gnashing of teeth—the sound of more laughter issued up from the waters of the pool.

So desiccated was the body that the spirit had left behind that by the time George Porter's corpse would be discovered several days later it would be unrecognizable. No form of identification would be found on his person (likely stolen by the person first stumbling upon him), which had quickly become a feasting ground for carrion.

Of the palace of Red Death from which Porter had come there would be no sign at all—or of any other structure. Only trees and stones and desolation.

With no true friends to notice his absence, it was a week before his harried employees reported him missing to the authorities.

By that time, his body had already been consigned to an unmarked, shallow grave in the city's Potters Field.

This avaricious man who had spent a lifetime accumulating wealth would end up in the company of paupers and derelicts—unmourned.

Nor would his wealth long survive him.

His equally rapacious relatives—his only heirs since he had forbade his longsuffering wife the joy of children—would assiduously devote their time and energy to having Porter declared legally dead so that they might descend upon his holdings like vultures on a carcass, picking it apart and leaving nothing of it behind save the bleached bones.

CHAPTER 15

"All we see or seem is but a dream within a dream."

Edgar Poe was sleeping but fitfully in the small bedchamber that had been assigned to him that first night.

He was dreaming of his father. His *true* father, rather than John Allan who with his wife had taken young Edgar in to raise following the death of the boy's mother and whose last name Edgar had adopted as his middle name.

Poe's mother Eliza couldn't help leaving him, having passed away from the consumption when Edgar was but a toddler.

But his birth father—an itinerant actor—had willfully abandoned the boy and the rest of his familial obligations.

As in all such dreams he had experienced throughout his life, Edgar saw the figure of a man standing atop a steep hill and knew instinctively that it was David Poe.

For the hundredth time, Poe attempted to run up the hill, a rocky and hazardous climb. At times he slid backwards and the palms of his hands grew slick with blood from clambering over sharp stones.

But he persevered until he reached the summit, stumbling toward the man who stood with his back turned, seemingly oblivious to the approach of the son. Drawing near, Edgar grabbed the man's shoulder and forcefully turned him around.

Only to see that the man had no face!

Whether it was this somnolent revelation that awakened Poe from his troubled sleep or the single, loud knock at his chamber door, he could not say.

He bolted upright in the bed and a few seconds later he heard two sharp raps on his door. Precisely five seconds later, three knocks sounded.

When, five seconds later, four knocks came, Poe had reached the door and cautiously opened it inward. Standing in the hallway without was the little dog man Reynolds, dressed in a fresh suit of cloths and looking rather perturbed and put upon (Or so Poe thought; emotions did not register quite as clearly on a dog's face and on that of a man.).

"Still alive?" the pooch sniffed. "Too bad."

Always cognizant and admiring of all things bizarre, Poe chuckled lightly. He was more of a cat person, yet still he reached out to pat the little dog man atop his furrowed brow.

His friendly gesture was rewarded by having Reynolds viciously snap at the offending appendage.

Poe quickly jerked his hand away as pain lanced up his arm. He looked down to see that the squat brute's nip had actually penetrated the skin, drawing two small droplets of blood.

"I'm not your *pet!*" Reynolds growled, furiously licking at the foam around his slobbery lips.

"Clearly not," Poe said testily. He brought the afflicted hand up to his mouth and sucked away the thin trickles of blood oozing from its pierced skin.

"Get yourself dressed," Reynolds ordered. "By the time you do, your breakfast will have arrived."

Poe did as he was instructed, taking great care for his daily toilette and dressing just as he always did; even in a situation as beyond the pale as this, he found he wanted to look his best. The last step was checking his appearance thoroughly in a conveniently available full-length mirror.

As Reynolds had said, within minutes one of the stork-masked servants appeared at the open door of the chamber. He brought with him a large tray well laden with breakfast foods: eggs, bacon, buttered slices of toast, a small bowl of sliced fruit and a carafe of juice.

"I'd advise you to eat well," Reynolds said as the servant left. "No other food will be provided until the evening meal."

Poe had already seen enough of the workings of this grim puzzle box to take the hound at his word, and ate heartily.

As he made ready to consume his final strip of bacon, though, he no-

...the man had no face.

ticed that Reynolds was eyeing the fried meat hungrily, licking at his foaming lips even more vigorously than usual.

"It's too bad that, as you so pointedly told me, Reynolds—you are not a pet," Poe said tauntingly. He held up the strip of bacon, letting it dangle in the air before his face.

"Otherwise, I would be sorely tempted to toss this last, juicy, succulent morsel to you."

Instead, Poe shoved the entire strip into his own mouth, making a great show of enjoying it to the accompaniment of smacking sounds and moans of pleasure.

Reynolds growled menacingly.

"Let's get going, then," he snapped. "The day is being wasted."

Happy to be started, Poe left the room and set off down the outside corridor in the direction Reynolds indicated.

As he set out at a brisk but steady pace, Poe engaged in mental exercises to divert his mind from the monotony of the large walk ahead. His thoughts turned to measuring his chances of completing the assigned trek ahead of the others. Although Red Death said that any and all who could complete the course would "win," Poe was not convinced he could be taken entirely at his word and felt it might behoove him to finish first.

He honestly felt that his chances of doing so were fairly good. In his younger days he had been quite an athlete, having on one occasion swum *six miles* up the St. James River. He was a champion long jumper and enjoyed both rowing and hiking.

Now in his 40th year of life, he was doubtless somewhat softer and less fit. Still, he felt certain he would have an edge over the two women, especially the even older Edna Benet. Reverend Farr was likewise older and carried a bit of a paunch.

The Southerner, Larou, was of the land—but not in the way of the true farmer who tilled and harvested with his own hands. Larou was a land and slave *owner*—accustomed to having work done for him and probably more inclined to ride than to walk.

Carp, the alleged highwayman, if he indeed had led the life of an outlaw, would possibly be adept at moving fast and far on foot.

He and Captain Montgomery—who at least at one time would have had to adhere to the physical regimen required of a soldier—would be Poe's stiffest competition in all likelihood.

Wishing to measure his own progress, Poe paused and checked his pocket watch. To his mild surprise and delight, he found that he had been walking for a full hour.

Yet, looking ahead, it seemed to him that he was not one step closer to the end of the corridor than when he began this trek.

Fearing that he had somehow been tricked into uselessly walking in place, he turned and looked behind him—and saw with relief that it did indeed appear that he had traveled some distance from the bedchamber in which he had slept.

Paintings hanging from the walls of the hallway and occasional small works of statuary that Poe had lightly noted in passing would also seem to preclude the possibility that he had been walking in circles.

He looked quizzically down at Reynolds, who seemed to know what was floating in his mind.

"Master Red Death *told* you the passage was longer than it appeared to the eye," the dog man said in an oily voice, his jowls turning up in the closest his canine features could come to a smile or a smirk.

"And so it seems," Poe said with a shrug.

"But where are the others—those I race against? I've seen no sign of them."

"That's because each is traveling his or her own path," Reynolds replied vaguely.

Those would be the last words he spoke for some time, refusing any of Poe's further attempts to engage him in conversation of any sort.

Initially, Poe was content merely to commune with himself, assuming that despite its deceptive length he would surely reach the end of the corridor before the day was finished.

But as the minutes continued to stretch into a succession of hours, he came to realize that the distance he had yet to go seemed scarcely to have diminished at all—even though, always as he looked back it appeared he had indeed traveled forward some distance.

"Have we been deceived?" he finally demanded of Reynolds, refusing to take another step.

"Have we been condemned to walk until we drop and die from sheer exhaustion? Is there truly no end to this damned corridor?"

"There is," Reynolds replied, breaking a silence that had persisted for hours.

"Though it is possible none of you will survive to see it." Poe thought the little mutt sounded extremely self-satisfied.

As Reynolds had warned that morning, no food was offered to Poe throughout the day's march, though periodically he would come across a leather bag of water hanging from a wall peg, from which he always deeply and gratefully partook.

The need for rest stops became slightly more frequent and lasted a little longer as the day progressed. There being no chairs or other sorts of furniture in the interminable hallway, Poe contented himself with sitting cross-legged on the floor.

During such times, Reynolds would simply throw himself down on his belly and had no trouble grabbing quick naps—always bounding immediately to his feet whenever Poe rose and continued marching forward.

At some point late in the day, Reynolds consulted with his own pocket watch, then snapped it shut loudly.

"That's it," he declared gruffly. "Today's march is ended. It's time for *supper!*"

The dog man licked his lips eagerly at the thought. Poe was also glad to hear of it. The hours of walking had left him both tired and famished.

From a vest pocket, Reynolds extracted a ring holding keys of various shapes and sizes. Fumbling slightly with them, he turned to unlock a narrow door set in the wall of the hallway—a door Poe would have sworn was not there but a moment before.

CHAPTER 16

Restraining his urge to rush on through the open door, Reynolds stepped aside and motioned for Poe to go first.

Stepping cautiously through the portal, Poe found himself standing inside yet another small banquet hall. (Just how many blasted rooms *did* this paean of peculiarity have? he wondered.)

At once he saw to his mild disappointment that all of his fellow contestants were already there—though apparently just barely, as they were still in the process of being seated by the servants.

At the head of the table, Red Death could be seen lounging in a slightly raised chair that was also larger and more ornate than the others around it.

Spying Poe enter at the back of the room, the masked man enthusiastically waved him over, and Reynolds ushered him to the chair at Red Death's right hand.

"So," Poe asked his host after taking his seat, "did we all then travel roughly the same distance today?"

"Not at all," Red Death replied. "Some made more progress than others."

He leaned closer and spoke softly behind one hand.

"You did quite splendidly, Mr. Poe!" He glanced over at the others. "The Right Reverend, not so well. Probably comes from spending more time on his knees than on his feet."

"How is it, then," Poe asked him in a normal volume, "that we all could end up here, at the same place and at approximately the same time?"

"Remarkable, isn't it?" Red Death quipped, straightening back in his chair. He and all his animalistic servants broke into mirthful laughter.

"Just another of the many mysteries this wonderful abode is wrapped within!"

"Whose chair is this?" the outlaw Carp inquired, ignoring the exchange between Poe and their host. Next to Carp, an empty chair had been tilted forward at an angle so that its back rested against the tabletop.

"Ah. That *would* have been George Porter's seat at our table this evening, had he not declined the invitation to join us in our frivolity."

"So he's most likely at home now," Captain Montgomery said. "Seated at his own table."

"Even more likely," Carp added with a smirk, "he's sitting in his office counting up the day's profits!"

"Wherever he is," Red Death said, "I'm sure he is enjoying his just rewards."

Something in the tone of the masked man's voice made Poe feel slightly ill at ease. He posed a question that had doubtless been on all their minds.

"This…remarkable place of which you are so rightly proud, sir. How did it come to be?"

"The way all things come about," Red Death replied. "It was made."

"And who made it?"

"Necessity."

"How long has it existed?"

"What year is this?"

"Eighteen hundred and forty-nine."

"Longer than that."

Poe stopped, certain that any further questioning would simply yield more such enigmatic answers. Some of the others persisted, though.

"It seems incredibly *wasteful*," Edna Benet sniffed. "The size of it, the grandiosity."

"It's no wider than the world," Red Death said.

"But what purpose does it all serve?" Justin Larou said pragmatically.

"Different purposes for different occasions."

"Forget the house," Reverend Farr said. "Who exactly are *you*?"

They could all hear Red Death chuckle beneath his mask. "Different things for different people."

"And who is your master?" Farr pressed.

"What makes you think I have a master, Reverend?"

"We all have a master, sir."

"Even He you call the master of all?"

Farr sputtered at this, unsure how to respond. Poe straightened in his seat, his interest in this verbal by-play rekindled by their host's answer.

"Are you saying you are *God*?" he asked.

In reply, Red Death reached over to refill Poe's wineglass. "I am simply your host, Mr. Poe."

Little conversation accompanied the remainder of the meal.

"An excellent repast," Red Death said at last, though, as the evening before, he himself had not partaken.

"Your assigned attendants will now escort you to your bedchambers. Please remember and heed what I told you before; it is the night that holds the greatest danger to you." He cast his eyes around the table.

"To that, I must add an additional warning. You must not leave those rooms, or even open their doors, until your servant calls on you in the morning. Keep your doors locked until then; do not so much as touch them." He tapped the top of the table with one finger.

"To do otherwise—will be to invite a horrible fate."

Total silence then descended upon them all, until at last the group of little dog men reappeared and directed them out of the banquet hall.

As he was about to make his exit, Poe paused and leaned back in to take a final look at their host.

Red Death was still seated at the table, holding a shiny plate up in both hands as if using its slightly reflective surface to gaze upon his own masked visage.

CHAPTER 17

A low, rumbling sound awakened Edward Carp from his sleep. Inherently ingrained with the mentality and instincts of an inveterate cutpurse, he aroused feeling suspicious.

Had some sort of wild beast been loosed in his bedchamber while he slept?

The growl sounded again, and now the highwayman chuckled, instantly recognizing that is had issued from his own grumbling stomach.

It wasn't the gurgle of indigestion, but more like the complaining of an empty belly alerting its owner of its needs. Small chance of that being the case, though, thought Carp. Lord knew he had consumed plenty of the sumptuous feast Red Death had provided them just a short time earlier.

He chuckled softly again. Maybe instead of lustfully eyeing the silverware at dinner he should have been filching a little extra morsel of food for later, as his keen thief's eyes had witnessed the penurious little woman Benet do when she thought no one was looking.

Feeling a bit dry in the mouth, Carp rose from the bed and, using the light from the flickering fireplace to illumine his path, walked over to the wash basin to pour himself a glass of water. As the cool liquid flowed down his gullet, his stomach issued yet another mild protest. He ignored its voice and turned back toward the beckoning bed.

As he did, he noticed something a bit odd. His shirt seemed to be hanging a tad more loosely than should be the case, as if it had somehow grown a size larger while he slept. Impossible.

A slight movement to one side was quickly revealed to be nothing more than his own reflection as he had walked past a mirror hanging on the wall. Suddenly curious, he stepped closer to it.

He normally spent little time looking at himself—usually no longer than it took him to shave himself. Still, it was naturally a familiar face that now looked back at him, though somewhat heavily shadowed due to the dimness of the light in the room.

Had the face belonged to another man, Carp would have instantly recognized it as being that of a thief. Birds of a feather recognizing each other, so to speak.

It was a look he had seen on the face of many a merchant and on every politician he'd had occasion to see up close. He wasn't sure about clergymen, having never been face-to-face with one until being thrown into the company of Reverend Farr in this quixotic quest of theirs. And he had mostly avoided looking too closely at Farr.

It was a nondescript face that looked back at Carp from the mirror. That was a good thing in his line of work, making it more difficult for the victims of his crimes to positively identify him for any pursuing authorities.

Carp frowned slightly as he ran a hand over his chin. His face seemed a bit thinner than he expected.

Not so thin as when he had been a boy, though. Growing up in the slums of Boston, hunger had been as constant a companion to young Edward as had been violence.

The source of both could be traced back directly to his shiftless, ne'er-do-well father. The elder Carp worked menial jobs only to slack his endless thirst for alcohol—the over-consumption of which frequently and inevitably led to the termination of those islands of employment.

To say Carp senior was a mean drunk would be to slather whitewash over the man's acts of brutality. Rather than direct his self-loathing at its rightful target, he blamed his inadequacies and failures on those around him and aimed his fury at his hapless wife and children.

Edward had suffered his wrath repeatedly and could still vividly recall images of his father standing over his cowering wife and children afterwards, bawling like a baby, begging for their forgiveness and swearing never to harm them again.

His pledges of reform were as fleeting and meaningless as his periods of gainful employment.

It was devoutly to be hoped that the monster was long since dead by now. Edward didn't know; having run away from home at the age of twelve, he had never again had personal contact with any of the other members of his family.

Just as vivid in his memory as the violence and nearly as hated was the *hunger* he often experienced as a child, also the result of his detested father's profligacy.

On more than one occasion, the family's entire sustenance for the day had consisted of nothing more than a small portion of a weak gruel Edward's mother made by pounding acorns into small particles and adding water. It was a special treat on such days if there had been sufficient firewood on hand to heat up this concoction, making it slightly more palatable than when served cold.

The first crime Edward had committed was when he rifled the pockets of a man who, unlike Carp senior, had done his drinking in a public house and passed out drunk on the street on his way home.

And the first thing Edward bought with his ill-gotten gains was a meal that filled his young belly nearly to bursting: a previously unknown sensation he found to be quite delightful.

A familiar and comforting smell wormed its way into his reveries, causing him to turn away from the mirror. The warm odor drew him to a table set against the wall on the other side of the room's doorway.

Sitting atop that table, resting on a pewter platter, was a thick slice of roasted beef. So fresh was it that wisps of smoke rose up from it.

Carp's mouth began to salivate heavily at the sight and smell of it. Impulsively reaching for the knife and fork lying alongside the plate, he sawed into the meat and found it had been cooked just the way he liked it: medium, with a hint of bright pink at its center.

With unusual eagerness, he forked a healthy chunk of the beef and raised it toward his lips.

His suspicious nature stopped his hand and made him question why he would have even considered consuming this morsel of meat.

After all, this tempting offering had not even been there until moments ago; of that he was quite certain. So, how had it come to be here now? More importantly—*why* had it so conveniently appeared to entice him?

To his conniving mind, there could be only one answer. It was a trick of some sort. The meat was doubtless tainted with some sort of poison or toxin designed to kill or at least greatly sicken him.

With a disdainful laugh, he dropped the fork and turned his back on the platter of roasted beef.

In response to his canny move, his stomach rolled rebelliously within him, clenching as if intending to punish his self-control by emptying itself in one way or another of what little there was of its current contents.

Willing it to quiet its protests, Carp threw himself back atop his bed. Recalling his impoverished childhood, he knew that sleep could at least temporarily blunt the effects of hunger.

Yet Morpheus seemed to have turned his back on the cutpurse, and sleep eluded him. The continuing smell of the roasted beef sitting untouched within reach seemed to fill the chamber and take roost within his nostrils. His hunger grew.

At last he flung himself out of the bed, heading not toward the beckoning beef but to the room's wash basin. If he could drink sufficiently, he felt, the water might at least fill enough of the hollow in his belly to assuage the beast gnawing at his innards.

As he raised a glass of the tepid liquid to his lips, however, he again caught sight of his own reflection in the wall mirror. He was stunned by what he saw.

The face staring blankly back at him, though it was unquestionably his own, bore the countenance of a man who had gone weeks without food! Its cheeks were so sunken they nearly met in the middle of his face. Only the faintest of lights flickered in eyes that exhibited little sign of life and none of hope.

Carp nearly doubled over as a fresh, stronger spasm twisted his middle. The pangs of hunger that screamed at him were louder than any that he remembered even from his deprived youth.

Feeling that he had no choice but to risk one means of dying over another, he staggered back toward the table where the suspicious beefsteak still awaited.

He lunged at the beckoning platter, only to recoil in disgust. The smell that assaulted his nostrils was no longer one of succulence but of putrefaction.

There was now damned little of the meat left on the plate. What little bits remained were of two colors. One was an almost florescent green, as of mold and rot.

The other was a sickly yellow-white—and was *moving*.

Swarms of maggots rolled atop one another, eager to get at scraps of rotten beef. What would have been toxic, possibly poison to Carp was a bacchanalian feast for the worms.

A sharp squeak brought his eyes to yet another participant in this dinner of decay. A *rat*, nearly as long as Carp's own forearm, sat on its haunches at the edge of the table. Its black, oily fur reflected darkly as its jaws worked at masticating a bit of rotted beef.

Crying out in despair, Carp fell back against the wall and slid to the floor, weeping in hunger.

He wiped his running nose on the back of one sleeve and realized his shirt now fit him even more loosely. He tore at the garment with bony, shaking fingers, popping buttons off as he ripped it open.

Looking down, he saw that his belly was now so concave that it nearly touched his backbone. Every rib was clearly visible, distending as if striving to break outward through paper-thin skin.

Driven nearly mad by this sudden and unnatural hunger that threatened to leave him starved to death, Carp allowed dark insanity to drive his actions.

With supreme effort, he pushed himself up on legs grown stick thin and weak. With slow, uncertain strides, he made his way back to the table whereon lay the remnants of the beef.

They were not the objects of his attention, however.

With the wall as support, he stood and gazed with wild eyes at the rat still squatting there.

Carp initially made no move, even holding his breath to keep his sunken chest from rising and falling. The moment he awaited arrived when the filthy rodent, largely ignoring the man already, turned its back to him to reach for another morsel of the rancid meat.

Carp cried out as he lunged forward, his hands closing around the middle of the rat. With answering squeals, it wriggled in his grasp, whipping its supple body back and forth. The outlaw felts its sharp teeth sink into his skin, but he refused to relinquish his hold.

He raised the rodent in the air, then slammed its head down on the edge of the table. The animal's efforts to squirm free increased and it now raked filth-encrusted claws down its attacker's arm.

Sobbing, Carp again brought the rat's head ramming down on the table. It went limp, but he took no chances and yet again bashed it down, satisfied by the sound of its snapping neck that it was now truly dead.

Clutching the furry carcass to his bosom as if it was the treasure of Croesus, he snapped up the sharp steak knife from beside the pewter platter that still squirmed with maggots and crawled closer to the light given off by the fireplace.

Though the pangs of the unnatural hunger had pushed him to the brink of starvation, Carp forced his fingers to move slowly and deliberately as he skinned and then gutted the dead rat, carefully scooping out its entrails and bowels so as not to taint the flesh with their contents and then tossing them into the fire.

It occurred to him to find something upon which to skewer the small carcass so he might roast it in those same flames. A new, more painful contraction of his stomach drove that thought from his mind. Like any other famished beast, he ravenously sank his teeth into the raw flesh of the rodent, its blood lubricating his throat and easing its passage down.

He halted his gorging only because his tender belly threatened to expel what he had devoured so rapidly. The outlaw focused on his breathing, willing his digestive system to calm and then halt its rumblings.

When it finally cooperated, he returned to his primitive feasting, devouring the rodent in less time than it had taken to skin it. With loud smacks the cutpurse licked his fingers and hands, lest any bit of fat or flesh escape his lips.

Still on his knees, he let his upper body fall forward until his forehead rested on the floor. A noise floated into his ear canals, nearly lost in the cracking and popping of logs in the fireplace.

It sounded, he thought, like the laughter that might issue from a child frolicking on a playground.

As that perhaps-illusory sound faded and disappeared—so too did the horrible hunger that had driven him to animalistic impulses. He pressed a hand to his belly and found that it was returned to its normal size and shape.

With the wall as his support, he pushed himself slowly to his feet and dared to once again look into the mirror.

The face reflected back at him had likewise returned to its normal color and fullness. The only thing marring its features was the look of shame and humiliation it bore.

Turning away from the mirror, Carp slid back down to a seated position on the floor, sobbing pitifully.

"God have mercy," he moaned softly.

But he didn't think God would.

CHAPTER 18

The bedchamber to which the dog man Reynolds had escorted Poe was similar to but not identical to the one in which he had passed the previous night.

The bed was different, having a high canopy above it. The blankets had been turned down and beneath it peeked out the edges of a ceramic chamber pot.

Flames crackled soothingly from a fireplace set into one wall. There was even a small writing table nearby. Still, Poe felt wary, on edge.

At least one of the other contestants would have no trouble falling to sleep that night. After a long day's walk, Edna Benet was exhausted and felt sure she would be able to slumber soundly.

Before retiring, though, she reached into a pocket of her dress and removed a small, wrapped kerchief. She then snacked on a piece of bread and bit of beef she had sneaked away from their dinner table.

She felt good about this, for she was certain that this perfectly good morsel of food would otherwise simply have been thrown away when the table was cleared. The thought of such waste was distasteful to her.

She even made sure to save a little, rewrapping it carefully in her kerchief. It would be welcomed during the continued trek that doubtless again waited on the morrow.

As expected, she was able to quickly fall into a deep and dreamless sleep after retiring to her bed.

Yet something awoke her in the middle of the night.

Edna lay in the dark, listening. It wasn't clear to her what the sound was that had roused her, though she thought it was a bit like that made by the scratching of a small animal's paws.

She rolled over to her other side, attempting to fall back asleep. But the soft noise persisted, denying her.

Growing annoyed, she sat up in bed and lighted a candle perched on the stand next to it. Even the pale glow it cast was sufficient to show she was alone in the bedchamber.

Still, she focused her concentration more intently, until at last she was able to isolate the point of origin of the sound. The realization brought her no comfort.

The noise was coming from the other side of the locked door leading into her bedchamber.

"Who's there?" Edna stridently demanded, throwing off her covers.

She took a step toward the door—and the noise stopped. Once again, her only companion inside the room was the sound of her own measured breathing.

"Mommy?"

Edna clutched at her constricting throat. Only the one word had been spoken and that in a voice she had not heard in years. Yet still she recognized it.

"Sarah?" she whispered in a hoarse voice, speaking the name for the first time in a decade.

It was the name of her dead daughter. The girl whom, though Edna tried to deny it even to herself, had appeared to her amidst the sickening swirl of souls inside the pool Red Death had shown them.

The sound of cold, dead fingernails scraping against the wood of the door resumed.

"I've missed you, Mommy."

Edna's eyes bulged in fear as she saw the knob on the door move slightly back and forth.

"Won't you let me in?"

Sinking to her knees, Edna clapped her hands over her ears in a vain effort to cut off the pitiful lamentations.

"I forgive you, Mommy."

With those words, long suppressed memories came flooding unbidden into Edna's reeling mind. They were memories of Sarah as a five-year-old child, abed and burning with fever.

Memories of Edna's weak-willed husband pleading with his steadfast wife to let him run and fetch a doctor for their baby.

But Edna had resisted his every entreaty. She had argued that it was pointless to spend hard-earned money on a condition she herself was perfectly capable of treating on her own.

Only, her own ministrations and simple home remedies had proven to be totally inadequate. Sarah's condition quickly worsened. Her writhing, feverish deliriums ceased only when she did.

Even while outwardly grieving her passing, Edna had still clung to her frugal ways. She insisted that the child be buried in the simplest, most inexpensive pine coffin available from the undertaker.

Shortly thereafter, Edna's spineless husband finally showed some intestinal fortitude for the first time—by leaving his parsimonious wife.

Edna had told the lie that he had died so many times and with such dramatic flourish that there were times when even she believed it was the truth.

"Please, Mommy," the weak, reedy voiced called to Edna through the heavy bedchamber door.

"It's so cold out here...so dark. Please let me in."

Rationally, Edna felt certain that she should ignore the plaintive entreaties. But emotionally, even a heart as strictly controlled as hers bid fair to break.

Slowly, very slowly, she found herself crawling on hands and knees toward the locked door.

"Hurry, Mommy! I'm scared!"

Haltingly, Edna's hand reached out toward the lock on the door.

Mere inches away...her hand stopped.

Edna yelped and jerked as an unseen hand on the other side of the door suddenly began to violently twist and pull on the knob.

"You *killed* me, Mother!"

The voice on the other side of the door, while still unmistakably that of little Sarah, had now grown harsh and accusatory in tone.

"You *owe* me!"

Edna's breathing quickened, as the yanking and rattling of the doorknob grew more violent, threatening to tear the very metal from the wood. Harder and louder it grew.

Then it stopped.

No more cries. No more scratching. No sounds at all.

Trembling as from the ague, tears of fear and sorrow rolling down her gaunt cheeks, Edna dared to move her face close to the door, pressing her eye against the keyhole set in the knob.

She saw nothing on the other side.

She pulled herself to a seated position, back pressed against the sturdy solidity of the door. Surrendering to her emotions, her breathing ragged, she began to sob softly.

She was taken totally unawares when a pair of small hands flashed through the door itself, to either side of her head.

She was able to scream even as nearly fleshless fingers closed around her throat and pulled back on her.

Edna was still screaming when, despite her thrashing struggles, those hands pulled her right through the door as if it was no more material than a curtain of smoke.

Then there was silence again.

CHAPTER 19

In the near darkness of his own room, Edgar Poe was awakened by the shrill screams of Edna Benet.

He bolted from the bed, the dim glow of the flickering embers in the fireplace providing sufficient light for him to race across the room. He was reaching toward the doorknob before he stopped.

He called to mind the warning Red Death had impressed upon them earlier that evening. To open their chamber doors before morning—was to court death.

Still, Poe bridled at the thought of doing nothing if a woman was in distress. His hand edged closer to the knob.

It could be some sort of trap, though, he surmised. It could be a trick whose purpose was to lure him to his own doom.

While he wrestled with indecision, the sounds of screaming grew fainter and fainter…and then stopped.

Realizing that any assistance he might have been able to render was now moot, with head hung he returned to the warmth of his bed.

Sleep was a long time coming and lingered only in fits and starts.

So it was that he was already out of bed and partially through his ablutions the next morning when he again heard the exact, precisely timed series of knocks sounding at his chamber door, growing harder and louder with each progression.

As expected, Reynolds was waiting in the hallway when Poe deigned to open the door. As was his wont, the dog man fiercely licked his jowls.

"Still alive?" the mutt said yet again. "Too bad."

The ensuing day's march down the still seemingly endless corridor was made worse by the fact that Reynolds now *did* see fit to speak to him—but only to taunt him for his perceived human frailties and to hurl insults and sarcasm in response to every comment Poe made.

Quickly tiring of this, the writer simply stopped talking. His breath, he felt quite sure, was better spent on aiding in his required physical exertions.

Still, Poe could not resist one more comeback when the dog man made yet another snide comment regarding the weakness and general inferiority of human beings in the chain of animal life.

"Yet a human is your master," Poe reminded him.

"No such thing!" came the gravely response.

"Then what is Red Death?" Poe inquired.

Reynolds made a huffing sound. "You don't really think he's *human*, do you?"

"Then, what is he?" Poe pressed, his curiosity piqued.

He almost succeeded in goading the dog man into an intemperate response. Reynold's jaws opened, then snapped loudly shut.

"He's the one who'll flay me alive it I don't keep you moving, poet. Step lively!"

Poe's own mouth stopped moving, though his brain continued to race frenetically.

Finally, as he knew it must, the wearisome trek was again called to a halt for the evening and as expected Reynolds again directed him through a concealed doorway and into the banquet room where the communal supper would be held.

Rather than stride straightway to the table, however, Poe held back long enough to clinically scrutinize the room, looking for any signs that it was the same location where they had dined the night before. If so, it might indicate that he and the others were indeed being tricked into simply walking in an endless circle.

But in addition to slight, cosmetic changes in the furnishings—the color of the tablecloth, the style of the chairs—he could also detect differences in the dimensions and configuration of the room, even in its beamed ceiling.

He felt that it was unquestionably a different banquet facility—and yet, once again he and all the others had arrived there at roughly the same time.

Red Death again awaited them, seated at the head of the table. As before, eight place settings lined either side of it.

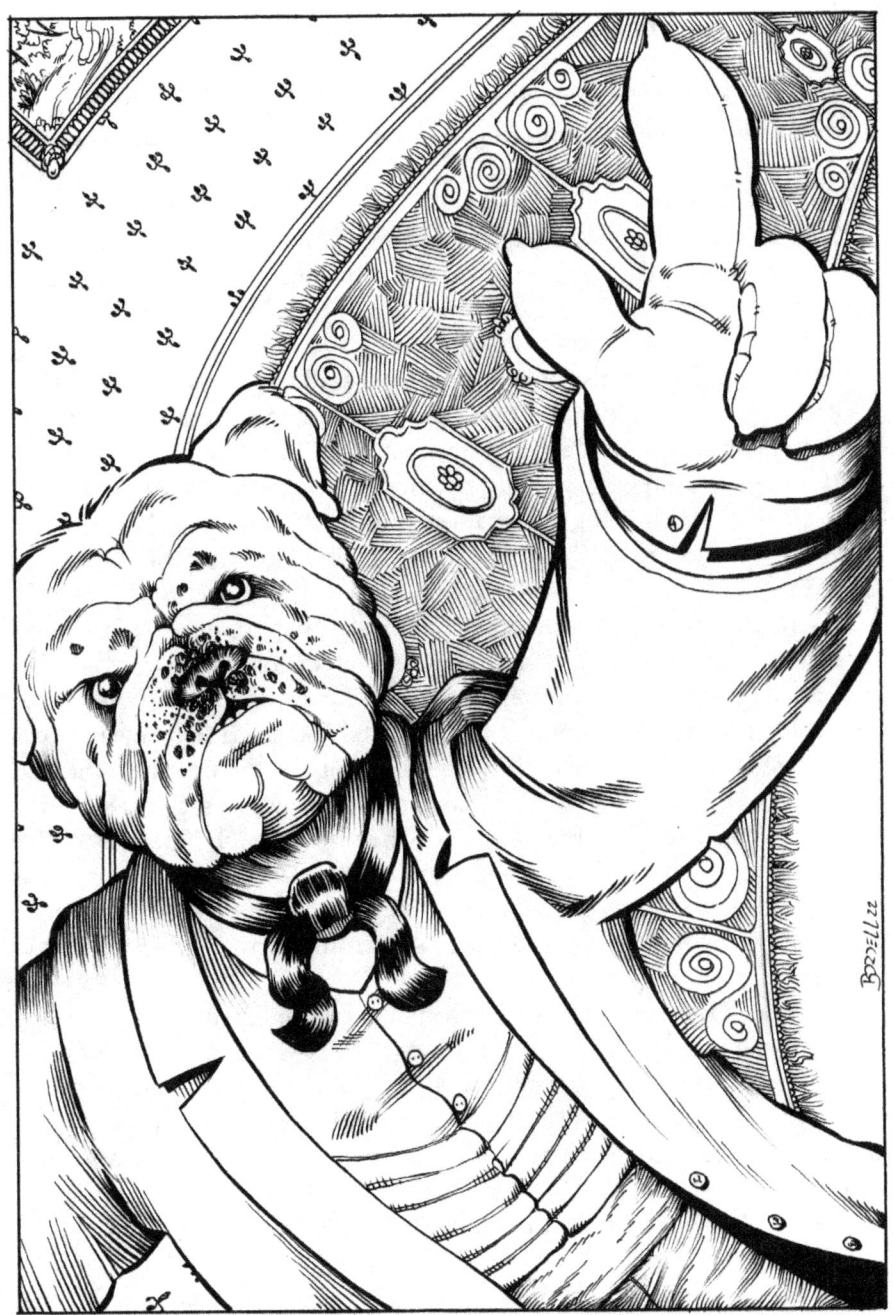

"...the one who'll flay me alive..."

But now *two* empty chairs had been tilted forward to rest against the table.

"I'm afraid poor Mrs. Benet is no longer with us," Red Death informed them, making a show of unfolding his large napkin and draping it over his lap.

"Some sort of…family emergency, I believe."

"She's *dead*, is what you mean!" Captain Montgomery exclaimed, grabbing for the freshly filled goblet of wine that had just been place before him by a servant.

Red Death simply shrugged in response.

"And it's too late for any of the rest of us to call a halt to this madness!"

Red Death languidly waved one hand. "You knew the rules when you agreed to participate in the game, my dear captain."

This time, Montgomery's only reaction was to take a large gulp of his wine. Poe found it passing odd that the military man among them seemed to be the one most deeply disturbed by what had presumably happened to Edna Benet.

If anything, he would have expected Montgomery to have had the most intestinal fortitude, the most stoic character of any of them.

"I must say," Red Death commented, wishing quickly to void the silence that befell the table by changing the subject, "you seem to be eyeing your *silverware* more voraciously, Mr. Carp, than you are the fine meal that has been set before you." The highwayman's only reply was a scoffing sound.

"He's probably calculating how much they would fetch if he was to filch them and sell them!" Candide Swan said snidely. Her cavalier attitude was mostly affectation, though. Whatever fate had befallen Edna Benet, Candide now knew that she would not be safe from harm simply by virtue of her sex.

"No doubt they're worth far more than the goods *you* peddle, girlie!" Carp snapped back at her. Seeing the looks of distaste on the faces of some of the others, he tried to smile his way back into their good graces.

"Actually," he continued in a voice as smooth as glass, "I was pondering how many meals could be purchased for poor folk for the price of this ostentatious finery."

"Tell me then, young Robin Hood," Red Death said, "is it the poor who benefit from the proceeds of your outlaw ways?"

"In large part, yes," Carp replied, abandoning any pointless pretense that he was not a thief. "Though I keep enough for myself to live on, naturally."

"Naturally," Red Death agreed with honeyed tongue. "And I must say you certainly make that mere pittance go a long way."

"What do you mean?" Carp asked.

"How else is it that you can afford the fine leather boots on your feet. Or the silk kerchief in your pocket?" Red Death paused for but a moment.

"Or your stable of blooded horses? Or the large country estate that you call home between your rounds of…charitable fund raising?"

Carp eyed him with hostile suspicion.

"He who pleases is of more importance to his fellow man than he who instructs," Poe added almost mischievously.

"I'm a simple man, friend," Carp said. The warmth in his smile was not reflected in his cold eyes.

"You'll have to speak more plainly."

Poe's returning smile was equally devoid of mirth.

"A man who eats steak while giving crumbs to the starving will still be seen as a benefactor."

Any semblance of civility melted from Carp's face and he clutched his steak knife more tightly, as if meaning to use it to slice a different sort of meat.

"Tell me, brother," Reverend Farr interjected, inadvertently defusing what was quickly escalating toward an explosive event.

"Do you also tithe to the church, as the Good Book exhorts us?"

Carp blinked, as if he couldn't believe what he had heard, then laughed raucously.

"Why would *one* thief donate his money to *another*?"

Farr, though clearly insulted by this remark, made no reply and the dinner descended into mostly silence.

Carp stared intently down at his plate, declining to start eating until he saw that the others were doing so. Reasonably sure that the food before them was safe to consume, he still hesitated. The memory of his great hunger from the night before made him fear that he would now descend upon his meal with overanxious zeal that might make the others suspicious. He forced himself to dine at a more normal, deliberate pace.

There was a minimum of small talk among the contestants until the meal was finished and the time came for them to again be escorted to their individual bedchambers.

"I urge you all to be especially cautious from this time forward," Red Death warned as they left the table.

"The respective journeys you are on may become more, not less, hazardous as they progress."

The warning—and the two unoccupied seats at the table—led them all to take the warning seriously.

CHAPTER 19

Poe lighted a candle upon entering his assigned bedroom, after making sure the door was locked, and scanned his surroundings. He quickly saw that it was similar but not identical to the one in which he had passed the previous evening.

Not feeling weary enough to go immediately to bed, he pulled up a chair close to the small fire already crackling in the room's hearth.

He sat there staring at the wildly dancing flames, enjoying a relaxing glass of wine. While perhaps not quite to the level of the true connoisseur, their masked host still showed good taste in the *vino* he provided his guests.

Poe imagined that, in another room, at this moment Reverend Farr might be engaged in his nightly prayers. Not being a particularly religious sort, Poe was unable to avail himself of such rituals and so, as was often the case, his thoughts instead turned inward.

This often proved not to be a good place for the author to go, prone as he had always been to bouts of deep and dark depression. He often tried to console himself with the notion that it was this emotional well from which he drew much of the material that shaped his writing.

But one can *drown* in wells, he knew.

The almost hypnotic flickering of the flames within the fireplace mixed with the mellow warmth of the wine and Poe's eyelids at last began to droop.

He was momentarily roused by a soft yet insistent sound.

A sort of moan.

Deciding it had most likely risen from his own breast, he disrobed and made his way to the beckoning bed.

In yet another of the nearby bedchambers, it was the not unfamiliar sound of heavy chains clanking one upon another that awakened the Southern plantation owner Justin Larou.

A heaviness in his limbs as he raised to a seated position in the bed led him to gaze down at his arms. To his surprise and consternation, he saw thick, iron shackles encircling his wrists, connected by an equally formidable length of chain more than a foot long.

Their design was well known to him, for they were of a design and make identical to those he used on slaves he was transporting to his homestead after purchasing them on the open market.

Larou took great pride both in his ability to recognize good stock and to make a good deal for its purchase. Some owners did little more than look at a Negro's teeth and give a perfunctory pinch or two to his arms before making an offer. Not so Larou; he checked over each perspective purchase as thoroughly as if it was a valuable draft horse. He especially enjoyed inspecting the physical virtues of the female slaves.

He'd never encountered one, male or female, that he was so taken with as to desire to part with an exorbitant amount of money for its purchase (with one notable and troubling exception, and he made conscious effort to give her no thought anymore).

Yes, Justin Larou was known from the slave markets of Richmond to those on the waterfront of New Orleans for his skillful haggling when it came to price, and no trader could truthfully claim to have gotten the better of him.

He sneered now as he gazed down in the dim light at the shackles binding him. They held no terror for him. Assuming that the little mongrel of a man who served as his guide would surely unlock them come morning, he felt sure they would not encumber him so much as to hamper in any significant way his slumber during the rest of the night.

The sound of an animal's growls coming from close by, on the other hand, did alert his senses.

It took but a moment's reconnoitering for him to detect two small points of light in the darkness beyond his bed, beyond the halo of light cast by the crackling flames in the fireplace. The points glowed red, as if they also were composed of fire.

And they were moving…coming slowly closer to his bed.

As they as last came near enough for the firelight to illuminate them, Larou saw that they were eyes, set on either side of a snout that ended in long fangs dripping with saliva. The massive, shaggy head of a four-legged beast came slowly into view.

"*Blue*?" Larou gasped in puzzlement. "Is that you, boy?"

It did indeed seem to be Larou's favorite hunting hound from back home. To have called it a dog would have been only half-accurate, for its heart also pumped the blood and the spirit of a wolf. Nearly as large as a colt, more than once it had brought down a bounding deer with its vise-like jaws before its master could get off a shot with his musket.

And more than once its fangs had closed around the limbs of another type of fleeing buck—on those rare occasions when one of the plantation's slaves had been foolish enough to attempt to run away.

Now, the hunter was here, in Larou's very bedchamber. The grayish fur that gave the hound its name bristled over bands of wild muscle that pulsed with every step it took toward its master. A menacing sound rumbled up from its broad chest, but Larou was unperturbed by it.

"Come to Papa, Blue," he cooed softly, giving the beast a warm smile.

In reply, the hound curled its upper lip back, baring fangs that were powerful enough to snap a plank in half.

"What's wrong, boy?" Larou asked cautiously. "What's the matter?"

His pulse quickened as he saw the hound's rear legs bunch beneath it; he knew what action usually followed from this posture.

With a roar akin to that of a puma, his once faithful hound launched itself through the air, its jaws open to grab and tear.

Larou threw himself off the bed, intending to make a run for the chamber door, the devil with Red Death's veiled warnings against leaving their assigned rooms after sundown.

He had taken only a few steps toward the door, though, when his right leg was suddenly yanked back. His foot flew from under him and he fell heavily to the floor.

Larou's first thought was that Blue had seized hold of him, but the truth he saw as he rolled onto his back was even worse. An iron shackle was locked around his right ankle, and it in turned was attached to a short length of chain bolted to the frame of Larou's bed.

The hellish hound threatening his life now stood atop that bed. The fur on its wide shoulders rose, giving the dog the appearance of even greater size. Its fangs were bared; the growl issuing from within and the narrowing of its intense red eyes gave the beast an even greater air of menace.

"Easy, boy. Easy," Larou said in a soothing tone, holding his hands up palms forward in what he hoped would be perceived as being a submissive gesture.

"It's me, Blue," he said soothingly. "You don't want to hurt me, boy."

In truth, the dog was devoted to his master. But Larou correctly surmised that this was not the real Blue at all, somehow magically transported here all the way from Georgia—but rather some beast come instead from Hell itself and only taking flesh in the image of the man's loyal hound.

The thought, the fear was confirmed when the creature leaped from the bed, its jaws agape with anticipation of sinking its fangs into the throat of the fallen man lying before him.

Driven by the innate will to live and acting on sheer reflex, Larou thrust both arms up and forward. Like the bit on a horse's bridle, the chain linking his wrists slid between the attacking beast's slashing teeth.

The hound's weight and momentum drove it forward to the point where its snout nearly touched the nose of the man before Larou was able to stop it. The impact of the plummeting beast came close to breaking his arms and he cried out in pain.

Rather than backing away, the animal tried to press forward, though the metal links of the chain between its teeth cut sharply into the edges of its mouth and prevented it from closing its hungry fangs on the man's twisted face.

Larou found himself inches away from the blazing red eyes that were but one sign of the beast's unearthly origin. It was as if beams of blazing light leapt from them and bored through his own eyes and into his brain.

His arms shook from the continuing effort to restrain the hound, and its muzzle drew closer to him. Thick, slimy slobber rolled between its teeth and where droplets of it fell upon Larou's exposed throat the skin hissed and burned as if by the touch of acid.

Larou began to fear that the hound would eventually gnaw its way through the chain itself. Redoubling his physical efforts, he slowly pushed the beast's head back by a few, precious inches.

He then lowered his right hand and raised his left in a single, sharp, twisting action. The hound yelped in pain as its head was yanked sideways. To ease the pressure on its neck, it rolled with the movement of the twisting chain. Its furry form fell off the man and slid across the hardwood floor, its sharp claws digging in to stop its momentum only with difficulty.

Larou used the momentary reprieve to regain his own footing and rise upright. Though still chained to the bedpost, he at least now had a modicum more freedom of motion to confront his attacker.

The hellish hound took its time, instinctively knowing its intended prey would not go down easily. Its corded body shifted back and forth from side to side, looking for any opening, any advantage. Larou aped its every move; his eyes always fixed on those of the beast that sought to drink deeply of his life's blood.

While moving primarily to left and right, the furred creature was at the same time inching slowly forward. The strategy was not lost on Larou, who had seen the real Blue execute such a maneuver many times back on the plantation—whether the prey he had brought to bay was a wild boar or a cowering slave.

That memory also brought renewed hope to Larou in his effort to survive this night. While the creature facing him was surely nothing more than a supernatural construct of some fiendish devising, everything about it—including every move it made—seemed to mirror exactly those of the true hound upon which this likeness was based.

And those mannerisms were well known to Larou.

So it was that he knew when the false hound was going to again try to pounce on him, a second before the beast actually uncoiled its hind legs and leaped, letting out a primordial growl as it did.

The natural move, the instinctive one, would have been for the targeted prey to either freeze in place or attempt to fall back; this was what the beast expected would happen.

Instead, Larou stepped forward into the attack. Having gripped the ends of the chain linking his wrists with both hands, he now swung it as a weapon, putting as much force into it as he could.

Its heavy links caught the hellish hound on the side of its enormous head, snapping it sharply to one side. To Larou's relief, he saw frothy blood and at least one dislodged fang fly from the creature's mouth.

Having been caught in midair, the hound now found itself falling to the floor with its momentum dissipated. Larou had no intention of letting it regain its senses and hence the advantage.

With a roar that nearly matched that of the hound in savagery, Larou brought his chain weapon straight down sharply. The beast yelped in pain as the iron struck directly against the top of its head. There was a loud cracking sound as its bony skull fractured and the beast crumbled limply to the floor.

But it was still alive—a condition Larou was determined to rectify. Grunting from the effort, and before the creature could make any move to retreat or defend itself, he brought the chain down again and again until the hound's head was little more than a bloody pulp of bone, hair and brain matter.

Convinced at last that the creature was destroyed, Larou fell heavily to the floor beside its unmoving carcass. Slowly, as his breathing returned to normal, he reached out and gently took the great, shaggy, bloody head in his hands.

"Poor Blue," he said softly, saddened by what he had been forced to do despite knowing that this beast was not in fact his true and cherished hound.

Moments later, as Larou looked on in astonishment, the creature's body began to change. It lost form and substance, transforming into something resembling shifting sand that filtered through Larou's fingers. Within seconds, even those bits of ephemera had simply disappeared.

With a metallic groan, the shackles on Larou's wrists snapped open and clattered to the floor. The same for that which held his leg bound to the bedpost.

Larou stared intently down at his now unencumbered wrists for several minutes, flexing his fingers from time to time.

He then began to chuckle. Then to giggle.

Then, falling back so he rested fully upon the floor, he began to laugh loudly, as if he had just gotten the point of the biggest joke in history.

CHAPTER 20

In yet another room, the outlaw Edward Carp knelt beside his own hearth, using a poker to stoke its flames.

Then he, too, heard a sound that put him instantly on the alert. No moan was this, though, but rather a high-pitched giggle such as might come from a woman.

Or a child.

Possessing the wariness essential to all in his dangerous profession, Carp leapt to his feet, casting his eyes about. At first he saw nothing, for even with the light being thrown out by the fireplace the chamber was largely enveloped in darkness.

A slight, almost imperceptible motion caught the periphery of his vision and he turned to see a shadowy figure standing in the far corner of the room. With a smooth, practiced move, Carp's hand dipped into the right hand side pocket of his coat.

"Come out into the light," Carp demanded harshly. "Show yourself like a man."

"But I'm not a man, am I?" a small voice replied even as the shadowy figure began to move forward out of the dark.

"And thanks to *you*—I never will be!"

The figure moved closer so as to be more fully recognizable. Carp was rather astonished to see it reveal itself as being a mere *boy*: one surely no older than eight or nine.

"You don't remember me, do you?" the boy said. He was close enough now for Carp to see him clearly.

Despite his obvious physical youth, there was an unmistakable deadness in the boy's eyes such as would usually only be seen in the very old or very ill. Well-used clothing hung loosely, slightly too large for his spare frame. Amber hair, thick and unkempt, topped his head.

"But you *will* remember me."

And in a dizzying flash that made his head spin, Carp found his mind swirling back to the events of a dark day now several years a'past.

Carp had often found it useful to pay and pay well for information that proved beneficial to him. It was through such means that he had learned of a wealthy merchant in Hartford who had an unshakable mistrust of banks and was therefore rumored to keep large sums of money in his own domicile.

On one particular early evening, the merchant returned to the home to find Edward Carp already there and waiting for his arrival.

He also found his cherished wife and household servants, tied, gagged and bound to chairs. Tears rolled down his wife's cheeks and her sobs, suppressed by the kerchief stuffed in her mouth, fair threatened to choke her.

And oh, how the moans and sobs had increased when Carp ran the barrel of his pistol softly down the side of her face as if it was the caressing stroke of a lover's hand. All to the impotent horror and outrage of her husband.

Carp placed his face next to hers, grinning coldly as he threatened to shoot the woman if her husband did not reveal the hiding place of his money forthwith.

The outlaw was impressed that, unlike some in the moneyed class that he had encountered during his endeavors, the merchant showed no hesitation at all in pleading for his wife's life in exchange for all the cash he had on hand; and it proved to be a substantial amount.

With a bag full of loot—plus the merchant's watch and he and his wife's rings and other bits of jewelry—Carp kept his word by leaving all in the house bound but alive as he quickly departed. So intent on fleeing was he that he paid scant attention to a small gaggle of children gleefully playing on the sidewalk outside the merchant's house.

The outlaw had been hasty and sloppy with some of his knots, though, and one of the household servants had succeeded in working his way loose. As Carp was reining his horse away, the impulsive servant burst out of the front door, rushing forward and rashly firing a wild pistol shot at the fleeing thief.

Though the lead ball flew wildly awry, the sudden sound of it and the reflexive tug on the reins caused Carp's horse to buck slightly sideways, spoiling the shot that Carp fired back in reply.

It was a shot that need not have been fired at all. Carp could easily have galloped out of range before the servant could possibly have reloaded his pistol and sent a second shot after him.

Carp's errant round flew well away from the offending servant who was its intended target, only to strike one of the nearby children—a little boy—squarely in the chest. From the way the boy stiffened and fell to the pavement, Carp had no doubt that the shot had been fatal. The child was dead almost instantly.

Yet here the boy now stood, facing his killer from across the room. Carp had thought he saw the boy's anguished face when he had stared down into the tangle of tortured souls within the Purgatory Pool—and now he was sure of it.

"What's my name?" the spectral little boy now asked.

"What?" It was a question Carp had not anticipated.

"What's my name?"

"How should I know?"

"You could have tried to find out. It wouldn't have been hard. How many other children were murdered that week?"

The fear that initially gripped Carp's heart at the sight of the ghost now mingled with anger. "Look, boy—it was an accident. You've got to know that I didn't mean to kill you."

"That don't make me any less *dead*, now, does it?"

"What's done is done," Carp snarled. "Go away, child. Leave me alone."

But the spectral waif continued to advance slowly toward him.

Carp's right hand came out of his coat pocket. It was now holding a small but potentially quite lethal British flintlock pocket pistol.

"Don't make me shoot you again," he warned, with a voice that quivered slightly.

"Do you think you can kill somebody who's already dead?" the ghostly boy asked. "Let's find out."

And he continued to walk toward the shaken highwayman.

"I mean it, boy," Carp said. There was menace in his tone, though the hand holding the pistol had begun to tremble noticeably.

"That's a smaller gun than the one you used to kill me with," the boyish specter observed, continuing to advance.

"It prob'ly won't hurt as much, will it?"

The boy was at point blank range when Carp pulled the trigger.

In the small, enclosed confines of the bedchamber, the report of even a small pistol's shot sounded like a veritable cannonade. A large puff of acrid black smoke propelled from the barrel of the gun, momentarily obscuring Carp's vision of his intended victim.

When the smoke did clear, the outlaw was stunned to see the boy still standing in front of him, seemingly unperturbed.

Yet he knew the shot had struck home; at this distance, he couldn't have missed. In fact, so close to him had the boy been that the spark from the flint's igniting of the powder had set the front of the child's shirt afire. It was but a small flame, which quickly sputtered and died, leaving behind a blackened hole in the center of the boy's chest.

A hole from which no blood flowed.

Carp's now empty pistol dropped from nerveless fingers as he gaped at the yawning wound he had inflicted.

Moments later, he saw that something *was* starting to squeeze out through the hole in the boy's body. Still, it wasn't blood; it appeared to be a small, solid object of some sort.

The object dully reflected the light from the fireplace. As it pushed out further into view, Carp realized with astonishment that it had the appearance of being a *gold coin*!

Once fully expelled from the ghostly child's body, the coin dropped to the hardwood floor at Carp's feet with a light, almost musical tinkle.

And right behind it, yet another coin was expelled from the wound. Then another and another. And ever more, coming out a bit faster now.

"That's the way of it, isn't it?" the ghostly boy asked rhetorically. "I'm worth more to you being dead than I was being alive, ain't I?"

Carp seemed not to have heard his words, though. Ever the outlaw, his eyes and his attention were now fully, hungrily focused on the pile of coins growing at his feet.

"You like gold, dontcha?" the boy said. "Well, there's lots more where that came from." He now had Carp's full attention once more.

"And you're welcome to all of it!"

With that, a grin appeared on the boy's face, spreading until his mouth was impossibly, preternaturally wide. A faint clinking sound echoed up from deep inside him, growing louder and louder.

Accompanied by a gagging retch, something shot out of the boy's gullet.

It was another gold coin. Such was the force with which it was expelled that when it struck Carp in the chest he winced with pain.

Then, as if this projected image of a long dead boy was literally vomiting gold, a heavy, seemingly inexhaustible spray of coins shot violently up from his innards and out of his mouth.

Like gilded bits of shrapnel they struck Carp in the face and torso. Crying out in pain he raised his hands up in self-defense, only to have his fingers ripped off. The flesh of his head and neck was quickly shredded into bloody strands. An eye was pierced and dissolved.

He heard the sounds of the ghostly boy giggling once more—just before that sound was drowned out by his own agonizing screams as his blackened life was torn away and his soul consigned to eternal damnation.

CHAPTER 21

Perhaps it was the wailing death rattles of Edward Carp that awakened Edgar Poe from his sleep: perhaps not. But by the time he was fully conscious, those sounds had faded to nothingness.

Once awake, he lay on his back, staring pensively up into space.

A space that strangely seemed to be less high above him than when he first had gone to his bed.

Initially, he thought the gloom seeming to close in on his was nothing more than the manifestation of the darkness that had seized his soul earlier that evening.

But the light still coming from the fireplace was just enough to convince him that somehow the canopy above his bed was now lower than it had been before.

The longer he stared at the blackness above, the more convinced he became that it was indeed descending toward him.

With a barely stifled cry he threw himself off the bed and onto the floor—just as spiky tendrils of darkness shot down from above. These spears of solid shadow came within inches of piercing his body from head to toe and pinning him to the mattress like a wriggling caterpillar.

To Poe's growing horror, the menace did not end there. The bulk of the nameless black mass dropped down from the canopy, absorbing the spiked tendrils back into its greater body.

Like a gelatinous glob of pure evil, it slithered over the side of the bed, oozed onto the floor—and began to flow like cold lava toward the stunned Poe.

Without rising, Poe crab-walked away from the ooze, until waves of heat lapping at his hands warned him he was about to back into the fireplace.

In desperation, he began frantically to thrust more wood into its flames, stoking the fire to make it burn more brightly and hoping that the light would repel the approaching dark.

The ooze did slow its progress, but did not stop its advance. Its ebony mass was mere inches away from Poe's foot and he had no doubt it could and would absorb him into its emptiness forever. In desperation, he pulled a flaming faggot from the fire and thrust it toward the horror.

The black tentacle closest to him jerked back as if afraid of the heat.

But, no, Poe thought. It was not the heat that had repelled it. As he had hoped—it was the *light*.

Grabbing a bundle of sticks and setting them alight, Poe cautiously advanced toward the dark mass, which slowly but continually retreated before their glow until it had slithered back atop the writer's bed. In the face of the unrelenting light, it had even shrunk in size and circumference.

Rising to his feet, Poe circled the room, igniting every candle and lamp he found. As the entire chamber at length became nearly as bright as day, the mass of black slime fairly leaped upward to press itself once more against the underside of the bed's canopy, the only remaining area of shadow of sufficient size to contain it as it sought shelter.

As a final move, Poe placed a pair of candles and their holders right atop the center of the bed, directly below the remnants of the dark terror.

He then quickly retreated to the corner of the room nearest to the fireplace, where he would be in position to feed its flames through the remainder of the night if need be.

As a last precaution, he placed two lighted candles on the floor directly in front of him.

Understandably, in the wake of this monstrous attack, sleep came neither quickly nor easily to Poe. Eventually, though, sheer exhaustion reached out its nebulous fingers to close his eyes.

"It's still too much about *you*, Edgar," a wispy, feminine voice that was almost familiar whispered in his ear just as he nodded off into a troubled sleep.

CHAPTER 22

As rosy dawn made her eagerly awaited appearance, Poe was jerked awake by the now familiar but no less irritating series of sharp raps on his chamber door.

"Still alive?" the dog man Reynolds said yet again as Poe opened the door to him. "Too bad."

So began another long and largely uneventful day. Poe had begun to experience a mild, scratchy rawness in his throat and drank more deeply of the strategically placed water bags in an effort to assuage it. The discomfort, he speculated, had been caused by sleeping, however fitfully, too close to the burning fireplace.

During one of his drink and rest breaks, he again turned to look back the way he had come. Gratefully, he could tell he had indeed traveled a good ways forward. Yet, looking ahead, he likewise had to admit that the end of the corridor and his journey still seemed impossibly far away.

Poe was ready, almost eager for this day to end, relieved when Reynolds once again led him through a magically appearing doorway into yet another small banquet hall.

On this occasion, Poe was the first to arrive; even Red Death was not yet on hand. The writer took the time alone to wander about the room, noting yet again that it truly was different than the previous rooms in which he had dined. One way in which if differed was a little table in one corner, upon which he found a small stack of books.

He idly thumbed through them but found that each was printed in a language he could neither recognize nor decipher. Each was bound in fine leather, but the pages had a texture and feel to them with which Poe was unfamiliar. A disquieting thought pushed to the forefront of his brain.

Could these books be printed on *skin*? And if so…from what animal?

"Hoping to find some hidden truth, Mr. Poe?" a voice suddenly said from directly behind him.

Startled, Poe dropped the tome he had been examining. He had not heard Red Death enter the room and was momentarily flustered when he turned to see the caped character looking over his shoulder.

He quickly recovered his aplomb, however, and smiled wryly.

"Happiness is not to be found in knowledge—but in the acquisition of knowledge."

"How astute!" Red Death complimented. "Please don't tell the others—but I wish *all* my guests were as witty and perceptive as you!"

"My thanks for the compliment, sir," Poe replied, realizing that vanity made his statement true.

"But, come now," Red Death said, making a sweeping gesture with one hand. "Dinner will be served shortly."

As he then stepped aside, Poe could see that the others were now in the chamber and preparing to take their seats around the table.

Again, all save one.

"Mr. Carp will no longer be gracing us with his charming company," Red Death announced, tipping another of the empty chairs forward to rest against the table.

"Why?" Candide Swan moaned, looking genuinely distressed. "Why in God's name did we all agree to submit to such suffering?"

"An excellent question, my dear," Red Death retorted, taking his customary seat at the head of the table.

"It does seem, at the very least, to display questionable judgement on your part."

He of course did not bother to impart on them the information that the one member of their party who *had* tried to excuse himself from the competition—George Porter—had also come to a terrible end.

"Never to suffer would never to have been blessed," Poe reflected philosophically.

"That's no comfort at all, Mr. Poe!" Candide snapped harshly.

"We all have our crosses to bear, young lady," Reverend Farr pronounced. "And we must not hesitate to shoulder them."

"We are all well aware of the Right Reverend's thoughts on this and other aspects of his religious faith," Red Death said, swiveling to his right.

"What are *your* thoughts on the matter of religion, Mr. Poe?"

"I've never really given it much thought," Poe replied deflectively, not wishing to be drawn into any such discussion.

"Which means you *have* given it *some* thought." This time it was the Reverend Farr who sought to press the matter.

"I'm sure we'd *all* like to hear what the great writer's opinion on the subject is." The tone of Farr's voice was unmistakably challenging.

"Very well," Poe said, pausing to fill his wineglass. "If you insist." This time, he did not smile.

"All religion, my friend, is simply evolved out of fraud, fear, greed, imagination—and poetry."

Red Death observed this exchange gleefully, with rapt delight.

"Some might call such thoughts heresy, Mr. Poe," Farr said with a deep frown. "Bordering on blasphemy."

"Only 'bordering'?" Poe replied archly. Now he did smile again, even as he lifted his glass to his sensual lips.

"What difference does any of that make where a scoundrel like Carp is concerned?" Justin Larou said. The plantation owner made a dismissive gesture with his knife before using it to cut off a generous piece of beef that was so rare as to still ooze blood onto his plate.

"Some might call such thoughts heresy, Mr. Poe."

"Good riddance to bad rubbish, I say." He popped the piece of red meat into his mouth and began to chew it vigorously with coarse smacking sounds.

"I wouldn't expect a slave holder to place any true value on human life," Reverend Farr sneered.

"What has one to do with the other?" Larou replied with disturbing frankness as he began to hack off yet another slice of beef.

"I buy and sell Negroes—not human beings. And I am acutely aware of their value on the open market at all times."

"You speak of them as if they are *livestock*," Candide Swan murmured, clearly troubled.

"That's exactly what they are, young lady," Larou responded as if he was instructing and ignorant child.

"Nothing less...and certainly nothing more."

With some effort, the conversation was redirected toward lighter subject matter until the meal concluded and the remaining contestants were ushered from the small hall.

Upon entering his own designated bedchamber, Poe immediately issued a deep sigh of relief.

The bed in this room had no canopy.

CHAPTER 23

"We know."

With a rather ungentlemanly snort, Captain Albert Montgomery awakened from his sleep.

It had not been a deep sleep; his slumbers seldom were, even when fueled by generous dollops of liquor.

Having awakened, he by habit reached for the glass he had filled with wine and set on his nightstand before retiring for the evening.

"We know."

Montgomery stayed his hand as he heard the whispered words that had roused him a moment earlier.

"Is someone there?" he asked softly, not sure if the voice in the darkness was genuine or merely the echo of a dream.

"We know."

Now fully alert, the military officer was certain that the voice was real. The hand that had been reaching for the wine goblet now instead curled around the butt of the Army revolver in the holster hanging from his bed-post. He didn't draw it, however, but let his fingers fall away from it.

He slid from the bed and lighted a candle. Lifting it and moving it from side to side, he saw nothing out of the ordinary revealed by its light.

"Dead," a voice seemed to whisper in his ear from behind. Yet when he spun around, there was no one to be seen.

"All dead," said a second voice, louder than the first and coming from a different spot in the room.

"Who are you?" Montgomery demanded.

"Why?" asked a plaintive voice that seemed to be that of a child.

"We know," a pair of voices responded from the darkness. These appeared to have come from women.

"Who are you?" Montgomery again snarled, his voice coming out at a higher pitch than he intended.

"Why are you here? What do you want?"

"All gone," yet another unseen haunt moaned. This voice was also female in timbre, but sounding older and more weary than had the first two.

"Who?" Montgomery cried out. "Who's gone?"

"My father," a child's voice replied.

"My husband," an invisible woman declared.

"My son," came the tired voice of the old woman.

"All gone," those and other voices said in unison.

Striding back and forth, waving his candle from side to side, Montgomery sought in vain to find the people from whom these strident lamentations issued.

"All gone! All gone! All gone!" The chant of the unseen voices grew louder and louder until Montgomery could hear nothing but them; he could not even hear his own screams as he yelled at the voices to stop.

Since those vocalizations seemed to come from nowhere, he had no way of making them cease their cacophony. At last he threw himself back on his bed, pulling his pillow tightly around him in hopes of at least muffling the voices.

It did him little good, for now they seemed to be issuing from inside his own head, echoing and reverberating off the walls of his skull and into the tissues of his brain.

Then a louder noise came to his covered ears, as if of a violent crash. Again leaping from his bed, he could see by the lighter darkness without that the wide double windows of his bedchamber had been thrown violently open.

Aeolian streams of air buffeted him as he moved to close the windows, slowing his steps as he forced his way through the gale. He took small comfort from the fact that its howling had at least momentarily drowned out the droning of the voices that had been assailing his senses.

After a seeming eternity of struggle, Montgomery at last reached the windows. Grabbing hold of each, he paused to peer over the ledge—and was nearly swept away by a wave of dizzying vertigo.

There was nothing but emptiness beyond the windows. It appeared as if this side of the horrifying palace of pain butted against a sheer cliff. Below it yawned a rocky chasm, punctuated by jutting, jagged outcroppings of solid rock. The floor of this crevasse must have been hundreds of feet below, for it was completely lost to the darkness.

The rational part of the soldier's brain told him this was an absurd impossibility. As incredibly large as this place had proven to be, there was no way it could be situated so high above ground. Nor could any such desolate chasm exist in the very heart of a city such as Baltimore.

But his irrational side, bolstered by the evidence of his own eyes, told him otherwise. It became even more imperative that he close the windows.

Before he could put action to the thought, though, he felt a sudden pressure at his back, as if multiple hands had been laid upon him.

With a force even greater than that of the opposing winds, the invisible hands began to push him forward, toward the opening in the window.

He resisted them, of course, but felt his feet sliding forward across the slick wooden floor of his room. When they struck the wall, he had no choice as to a course of action; he could either step up onto the beckoning ledge of the windows or allow his body to topple over it and down into the void.

The thought of bouncing off the rocks below, bones shattering like kindling at each point of impact until he would doubtless be long dead before his body reached the floor of the canyon, filled him with a dread such as he had felt only once before in his life.

Montgomery stumbled up onto the ledge, but his fingers nearly dug into the solid wood of the window frame as he fiercely fought against being pushed into oblivion.

"What do you want?" he wailed in a pained and pitiful screech.

The whispered reply that tickled his ear was made all the more terrifying in that it appeared to come from the lips of a small child.

"We want you to die!"

The pressure of the many hands seeking to topple him to his doom grew stronger. Montgomery's breathing was ragged as he stared down at what would be certain death.

His will to live was as strong as his fear of dying, but still it seemed to be not enough. His nails now dug into the window frame so hard and so deeply that his fingers bled. With his legs, he pushed back against the ghoulish hands shoving him forward.

He cried out, as the pressure against his back suddenly seemed to break. No longer meeting any counter resistance, the soldier's body was flung back into the chamber proper.

As he lay curled in a ball on the floor, the howling winds reversed their course. They were sucked out of the room, dragging with them the ghostly chorus and slamming the windows shut as they made their final exit.

For nearly half an hour, Montgomery remained curled up on the floor. Only then did his breathing return nearly to normal. Finally, rising only as far as his hands and knees, he began to crawl frantically back toward his bed.

It was not the solace of its covers he sought. It was not the handle of his revolver for which he reached with shaking, outstretched hand.

It was the comfort of the wine bottle that had miraculously remained upright and intact on his nightstand.

Its liquid courage was what he most desired at the moment.

CHAPTER 24

In his own bedroom, Justin Larou was relaxing before the warm fire and enjoying a bracing glass of cognac.

He leaned back into his plush easy chair, exhaling contentedly and closing his eyes. For all the madness this strange place embodied, he thought, for all the dangers it presented—it did provide its occupants well with the creature comforts of food and spirits!

So relaxed did he become in these luxurious surroundings that he initially thought nothing of it when he felt a firm yet tender pair of hands take hold of his boots and skillfully slip them from his feet. After all, this was just the sort of personal service he would have expected one of his house slaves to perform for him.

But he had brought none of those slaves with him!

Larou's eyes snapped open in fear and suspicion, but his expression quickly changed to one of mere surprise when he looked down at the floor in front of him.

"*Althea?*"

Kneeling at his feet was a familiar young woman. Her simple cotton shift did nothing to conceal the full, nubile curves of her mature body.

A *quadroon*, her bronze skin that fairly glistened in the reflected light given off by the fireplace was barely darker in tone than was Larou's own.

The planter remembered well that he had been smitten by her smoldering, sensuous beauty from the moment he first laid eyes on her in a New Orleans slave market. He would gladly have paid double what he did to make her his property.

Back home at his Georgia plantation, the woman had quickly become his favorite—after having been even more quickly taken into his bed.

Larou smiled, delighted to see the woman here, now—especially when she began to run her talented fingers slowly up the inner part of his thigh.

For the moment, at least, he was willing and able to ignore the fact that the woman kneeling at his feet—was *dead*.

Though the vision he now beheld was only that and nothing more, it mirrored the image Larou had glimpsed while gazing down into Red Death's pool of souls. It was an image that brought him a sense of longing such as he had never experienced.

In a separate bedchamber, Edgar Poe stood staring into the gleam of his own fireplace, lost in thoughts of the day just past and of days long gone.

Such ruminations ceased when a gentle tapping sound intruded upon them. The rapping seemed to be coming from outside the heavy, leaded windows set in the opposite wall of the room.

His curiosity aroused, he crossed over to the double windows, listening more closely to the staccato sound.

Poe's hands reached out to the twin latches, then stopped before twisting them. As he had witnessed firsthand, nothing in this macabre palace was as it seemed and danger could lurk in many forms and in many places.

But his innate, questioning nature got the better of him. After all, their strange host had warned them not to open their doors at night, on pain of death—but he had issued no such warning about *windows*!

Poe tightened his grip on the latches and in a single movement flung the windows open –

To see nothing but the blackness of the night beyond. There was no moon, no stars evident: not even the city lights one might have expected to be visible at least at a distance.

Then a loud squawk startled him.

His eyes rapidly adjusting to the inkiness, the writer saw a large, black bird perched on one side of the outer windowsill. Its head was tilted at an angle, its dark, unblinking eyes studying the man.

Nearby, the enthralling slave girl Althea slowly slithered her way up Larou's legs until she made her way into his welcoming lap.

Her lithe, well-muscled arms snaked around his neck and pulled his face down toward hers. Her kiss was as wet, warm and inviting as he had remembered.

As Larou felt himself becoming fully aroused, his hands began to explore the woman's inviting body. The sense memory of having done this on many past nights threatened to overwhelm him.

But then reason, for just an instant, prevailed over lust. Grabbing the woman's arms, Larou not ungently pushed her back away from him.

"This can't be happening, Althea," he said in a whisper that was almost a croak. "You're dead!"

"Yes, I am, Marse Justin," she replied in a voice flecked with ice.

To Larou's disappointment, she slid off his lap and back down onto the floor, coming to rest once more at his feet.

"But you wouldn't know much about my death," she said, her eyes now burning into his breast. "What with you sittin' in that fine old house up on the hill while I was dyin' down in the filthy slave quarters.

"Oh, and it were a horrible, painful death, too—givin' birth to the baby you planted in my belly."

"I didn't know what you were going through," he said lamely, not even believing the words himself.

"You didn't *want* to know!" she snarled. Larou reacted as if she had physically struck him.

"I begged, Marse Justin," Althea's ghost moaned, rocking back and forth. "And then I screamed. I screamed for God to help me and I screamed for you....

"But neither of you helped me."

"I did come to you," Larou said defensively.

"Oh, yeah, you came at last—after one of the field hands done went and told you I'd delivered you a *son.*

"But by then, it was already too late for me—and too late for my baby."

"What do you mean?" Larou asked in puzzlement. "The boy came out just fine."

"He did, didn't he?" the specter said wistfully. "And he was beautiful, too;

I lived long enough to know that.

"And the last thing I did, 'fore I took my final breath, was to make you promise to take good care of him."

"And that's what I did," Larou replied stiffly.

"Oh, yes," Althea said coldly. "You fed little Jacob, you clothed him. You growed him up into a good and strong and handsome young man." Her voice trailed off.

"And then you sold him."

Larou tensed, his lips became little more than a slash in his face. "That was just business, Althea," he stated, though his voice lacked conviction.

"It was nothing *personal*."

"Maybe you're right," the ghostly slave girl said, growing suddenly demur. She scooted a little farther away from Larou, but held her arms out to him invitingly.

"And maybe you'd rather think about *other* things, Marse Justin."

Larou licked his lips in anticipation of the delight that was being offered to him, tasting the moistness of her first kiss mixed with tiny droplets of cognac. He slid forward in his chair, began to lean toward her.

As he did, Althea's arms dropped down to her sides. Her eyes had taken on a cold, accusing glare.

"Do you know how *he* died?"

Before he could process the question, Larou heard a sharp crack a split second before a searing pain ripped through his back. He shrieked in shock as the searing agony caused him to lunge out of the chair involuntarily and end up on his knees on the floor.

He lifted his head to find it mere inches away from Althea's. He could see no lust now in the woman's eyes, no mercy.

"My boy, my baby," she hissed, "was *whipped* to death by the monster you sold him to!"

As a soft, scraping sound tickled his ears, a panting Larou cast a stunned look back over his shoulder.

From out of the chamber's shadows, a young man—really little more than a grown boy—strode forward confidently. Save for a slight kinkiness to his hair, he had all the appearances of being a white man.

His handsome face combined the finest features of both Larou and his mother Althea. His body was tall, lean and muscular: shown off to full advantage by the fact that the only clothing he wore was a brief loincloth around his middle.

"Say hello to your *son*, Marse Justin!" Althea practically howled. She began to laugh, but the sound quickly faded away—as did she, until she had completely disappeared from his sight.

"Don't go, Althea!" Larou cried in vain. Tears of pain and shame welled up in his eyes. He again looked back over his shoulder, to see the ghostly image of his dead son approaching.

As the specter stepped closer, Larou was able to see some of the signs of the whipping to which Althea had alluded. There were raw marks indicating where the lash, after striking the young man's back, had partly snapped around to lance the flesh of his shoulders and chest.

The ghost turned his head slightly to one side. Larou flinched as he was now able to see that Jacob's scalp had been laid open, his handsome features distorted and partially hidden by a loose flap of red, bloody skin hanging down from the laceration.

Without saying a word, the specter then turned around. Scalding bile rose in Larou's throat at the sight of his son's back.

It looked like a raw carcass that had been worked on by a drunken butcher. Having literally been flayed alive, the young man's flesh—where it was not entirely missing—hung behind him like angry, bleeding ribbons. The gaping wounds revealed that the lash had penetrated deep enough to lacerate muscle and tendons as well. In several places, the light from the fireplace dully danced off exposed, blood-spattered bone.

Larou had no doubt that young Jacob had been hours in the dying, with each second of it being one of unspeakable anguish.

The ghostly mulatto slowly pivoted around again to face his father.

"Do you know what my 'crime' was?" he said. His voice was raspy, for the whip had even lacerated his throat.

"Do you know what horrible deed I committed?"

Larou found himself unable to reply.

"I stole a *ham* from the massa's smokehouse. It was just a little ham… barely enough for the ten of us field slaves to have a bite or two.

"But the man you sold me to decided a lesson needed to be taught. An example had to be made.

"*I* was the example."

Again, words eluded Larou. His eyes widened slightly as he only now spied an object clutched in Jacob's right hand. It was a coiled bullwhip, such as must have been the instrument of the young man's own torture and death. It was doubtless its sting that Larou had felt moments earlier.

Releasing part of his grip, Jacob again allowed the whip to uncoil onto the floor.

"No!" Larou shouted, at last regaining the use of his voice.

It was too late, for the specter's arm flashed back and then forward, flicking the tip of the whip out and down.

Larou shrieked as the lash laid out across his left shoulder with enough force to tear through the cloth of his coat and the shirt beneath it, laying open the exposed flesh.

Larou's hand flew up to the laceration and he toppled over onto his side. As he lay on the floor, Jacob stepped in closer.

His left hand grabbed the rent cloth of his father's coat and pulled roughly. Larou struggled, but was unable to stop the specter from viciously tearing away at his clothing. He didn't stop until the planter's entire upper body lay naked and exposed beneath him.

"What would be fair, Father?" the ghost asked him. "What would be the just punishment?" Jacob's voice was cold and empty as the grave.

"I'm thinking one lash for every dollar you pocketed from my sale."

"No," Larou whimpered, knowing full well no man could possibly survive that many bites from the bull. Jacob raised the whip high over his head.

The ensuing blow tore across Larou's face, nearly ripping his nose off. Jacob's arm rose and fell rapidly and methodically. Leather tore again and again at his sire's wildly wriggling body.

Blood sprayed as the lash parted flesh, tearing it nearly from the bone beneath. A lancing slash across Larou's midsection nearly disemboweled him. Gore bubbled from the planter's mouth, the shock of the whip denying him the release of losing consciousness. The sounds that issued forth were barely human.

But Justin Larou's animalistic screams of agony stopped well before the whipping did.

CHAPTER 25

This time, Edgar Poe was unable to hear the cries of the slave owner through the walls of his own bedchamber.

His attention was focused on the black bird that was perched on his windowsill. To his delight, it made no effort to take flight as he slowly stretched his hand forward and stroked the slick, glistening feathers atop its head.

"One of your brothers brought me fame," he told the bird. Then his features darkened.

"And I brought myself shame."

His mind carried him back a few years, to the publication of his poem, "The Raven."

For reasons perhaps unfathomable, it had caught the fancy of the often-fickle public. Virtually overnight he became a literary figure of great renown.

He smiled at the memory of occasions when children would recognize him on the street as he strolled along. They would rush to cavort around him, joyously flapping their little arms like wings and imitating the caws of the black bird.

Those were good times: the deserved byproduct of years of literary labor. He had relished in them.

But then the pendulum of life had swung to the dark times.

He had engaged in a torrid but illicit affair with another writer: the poetess Frances Osgood, who was like Poe married to another. Through the conniving of another, spiteful woman whose own amorous advances Poe had rebuffed, his affair with Osgood had become rather common knowledge.

There always existing that perverse desire within the collective bosom to tear down the very idols they themselves had erected, public opinion had begun to turn against Poe for his infidelities.

These negative feelings toward him were exacerbated by the response to written criticisms Poe had leveled against Henry Wadsworth Longfellow. Poe had gone so far as to accuse the hugely popular poet of the creative crime of plagiarism. As a result, the great unwashed had directed their ire not at Longfellow but at Poe.

The emotional *coup de grace* against Poe came with the death of his wife. Long-suffering in more than one sense, Virginia had persevered valiantly before her inevitable loss in her battle against consumption.

A flapping of wings brought Poe's mind back to the present. As he watched, a second black bird fluttered down onto his windowsill to join the first. It looked slightly different from the other, and Poe considered the possibility that technically it might more accurately be a crow rather than its close cousin the raven. Still, he greeted it with a smile as well.

Then a third ebon-winged bird joined the gathering. And then a fourth.

As they all swiveled their feathered heads to stare at Poe, the smile that had tugged up the corners of his mouth diminished slightly. It had popped into his head what the term was that was used to describe a flock of crows.

A *murder*.

CHAPTER 26

Still not unduly concerned, Poe again reached out to stroke the shining head of one of the black birds perched on his windowsill.

This time, however, the avian struck at him with its pointed beak.

Poe jerked his hand, his whole body away, shaking the appendage against the stinging pain. He then stepped back toward the window, intent on closing its panels on his now turned hostile visitors.

As he moved closer, though, his eyes were drawn toward the horizon. The night had suddenly grown darker, as if a broad black cloud had descended from the heavens to shut off completely even the faintest of celestial lights that might have been trying to gleam.

He quickly realized that this "cloud" was rapidly moving closer, like an ebon, rolling ocean wave. As it drew nearer, a harsh sound began to emanate from it.

It was the sound of birds cawing.

Poe frantically reached for the twin panels of the window, meaning to slam them shut and latch them closed. But the rolling tide of blackness struck quicker than he could have imagined.

Without slowing their flight in the least, a flock composed of scores of black birds crashed into the bedchamber like a feathered battering ram. Poe was thrown backwards, tumbling to the floor.

He scrambled to his feet as quickly as possible as the birds began to swirl around him. He threw his arm up to protect his face as the maddened avians' rapacious beaks and flashing talons instinctively sought to tear out his eyes and rend his flesh.

Poe began to flail about, hoping to scatter his attackers, but they were undeterred. Every one he managed to swat aside was quickly replaced by two others.

His vision blurred slightly as the blood from a facial laceration rolled down into his eye. He may have screamed from fear and pain, but if so the sound was drowned by the piercing screeches of the birds. Their hungry cries assaulted his senses, drilling through his ears and into the very core of his racing brain.

One pain fell fast upon another as his flesh was laced with red furrows that quickly filled with his blood. A striking beak barely missed piercing his left eye, though it still left an oozing hole in his forehead.

He began to spin in tight circles so as to present a moving target for the scavengers turned predators. One landed on his back, raking at the exposed skin of his neck.

In a bit of irony lost on the author at the moment, Poe's swirling gaze fell upon the small writing table that was part of the chamber's Spartan furnishings.

More specifically, upon the wooden *chair* beside that table.

Staggering forward, pushing his way through the murderous flock by sheer force of will, ignoring the growing pains as best he could, Poe made his way to the chair, grabbing it and lifting it off the floor.

He swung the chair with wild abandon, crying out at the mild victory of feeling its firmness make contact with small, feathered bodies.

Yet while some subsequently fell to the floor, most were able to fly up and away from his improvised weapon. Some, like the waters of a river diverting to either side of an obstructing rock before continuing their journey, simply flowed around him and began to attack him from behind.

Crying out wildly, Poe swung in a complete circle, the heaviness of the chair making his arms ache but also clearing a swath around him.

Realizing he could not keep this up for long, and with the pounding screeches of the birds threatening to push him over the brink of sanity, in a last desperate move Poe flung the chair at the hovering, feathery cloud. As the birds dispersed briefly, the man made a mad dash back to the open windows.

Poe leaped atop the sill, and to an observer it might have appeared that he intended to end his tribulations by leaping to his possible death.

Instead, balanced atop it nimbly, he turned back to face toward the interior of the room, standing on the sill with arms akimbo.

"You want me?" he screamed at the birds in a taunting voice rising to an almost maniacal level.

"Come and get me, damn you!"

The flock of black birds hovered in the air momentarily. Then, as if acting on the directions of a single, united mind and with a great screeching sound, flew to the attack.

As though hypnotized by the glistening of black, flapping wings, Poe simply stood and stared as though transfixed, entranced by the feathered wave of death hurtling toward him.

At the last possible second, he lunged down, throwing himself flat on the floor. The cawing cries of the birds and the beating sound of their wings deafened him to any other sound as they flashed by just above him, hurtling through the opened windows and out into the night air.

The instant the maddening sounds moved past him, Poe bounded back to his feet, intent on closing the heavy windows against the flock's inevitable return. Already, as he grabbed hold of the twin panes, he could see the birds frantically wheeling in the sky to circle back toward their chosen prey.

The first of the birds reached the opening before Poe could get the windows fully closed, slamming their pinioned bodies against the heavy glass like suicidal moths drawn to a flame.

Poe braced himself, pushing forward with all his might as even more of the black birds strove to enter. Such was the force with which they struck the windows that the glass became speckled with their blood.

They were clearly willing to die to reach him. Could he exert any less effort to live?

A feathered head slipped through the narrow space between the two windows, furiously pecking at Poe's fingers. He cried out in pain and felt his feet slide slightly out from under him.

With a savage cry springing from his tongue, Poe desperately threw his shoulder against the windowpanes. At last they closed sufficiently for him to throw the latched that would lock them in that position.

Panting for air, his heart pounding in his breast, he took a few steps back.

The birds continued to hurl themselves madly against the glass barrier. To Poe's consternation, he saw small cracks appear in the thick panes, their web-like fissures running with the blood of birds that had killed themselves in the effort.

Finding it hard to think amidst the cacophony of the birds' screeches and the pounding on the glass, Poe cast his eyes toward the door of his bedchamber.

If he was on the other side of it, he felt certain, its heavy wooden bulk would be sufficient to spare him from further attack by the menacing black birds.

But, if Red Death was to be believed, it might also expose him to even greater, more horrific peril. He found himself torn by indecision. He pressed his fingertips against the sides of his head, even as he stood no more than a step or two away from the door.

He paused.

Had the sound of the birds pounding at the window diminished?

No.

Yes.

Slowly at first, then more rapidly, the sound of bodies striking glass lessened. The caws grew fainter. At last, there was no other sound than that of Poe's panting.

His knees turned to water and he dropped heavily to the floor, falling over onto his side.

It was while still in this position that he fell asleep.

CHAPTER 27

When Edgar Poe awakened in the early hours of the following morning, his brain felt befuddled to the point where he wondered if the harrowing events of the previous evening had been nothing more than a feverish dream.

The stiffness he felt all over upon rising—coupled with the sight of several dead black birds sprawled out on the floor—convinced him as to their reality.

On wooden legs he stumbled to the wash basin. Tipping it over so that loose feathers tumbled from it, he filled it with the contents of a water pitcher. Dabbing gingerly with a moistened cloth, he cleaned dried blood from the many, fortunately superficial lacerations on his hands, face and neck.

Nearly more distressful to him was the discovery of several small tears in his coat and shirt. Being usually an impeccable dresser, this caused him much consternation.

His throat burned slightly at the sting of cool water he sought to drink, and he found he had some difficulty swallowing it.

He had neither time nor inclination to pay heed to such discomfiture, for at the moment the dreaded but expected series of staccato knocks began at the door of the chamber.

"Still alive?" Reynolds growled upon seeing the door swing open, his repetitious greeting growing rather maddening.

"Too bad."

"You know, you beastly little mongrel—there are people who *eat* dogs," Poe snapped, pushing past the pugnacious escort and out into the beckoning hallway.

"Let them try!" Reynolds snarled, rushing to catch up with his charge.

Yet another uneventful day of hiking followed for Poe. He failed to see the point of it, unless its purpose was simply to challenge the contestants physically and by so doing also stretch the limits of their intellect. Still, he continued to press onward.

Doggedly so, he thought with a smile. He gave no voice to the pun, however, certain that his canine companion would fail to comprehend it.

The soreness in his throat persisted throughout the day and Poe also found himself perspiring more freely than on previous days.

Though it pained him to admit, he suspected this was due to the fact that, at age forty, he was probably not as physically fit as he had been in his younger and more athletic days.

He was more than ready when Reynolds signaled the end of the day by once again ushering him into the hall that would house that night's dinner.

As he had come to expect, Poe saw that yet another empty chair now rested on edge against the table: that which otherwise would have been occupied by the plantation owner Justin Larou.

"Please, sir," Reverend Farr said, directing his attention toward the already seated Red Death. "Before this madness goes any further—tell us what fate has befallen those who are no longer with us."

"I'm afraid they weren't up to all the challenges they faced," was all their enigmatic host said in reply. Poe wondered if, like him, the others had been confronted with multiple attacks upon their lives and sanity.

Only now, he realized with some shame, did he take the time to look closely at his fellow contestants. More than one, he saw, like him bore the marks of some physical struggle: a bruise here, evidence of a cut there. He realized that they, too, must have faced down their own horrors more than once—until, one by one, some of them had succumbed to their nightmares. His eyes could not see what wounds their psyches might have sustained. Probably, again like his own, these ran at least as deep as did the purely physical ones.

He feared this might portend even greater horrors ahead, but all he said for the others' ears was, "There are some secrets that do not permit themselves to be told."

"Well said!" Red Death complimented the author.

"And I'll just bet you have some juicy ones of your own, Mr. Poe!" Candide Swan said, her words accompanied by her trademark giggle.

Poe's only reply was a smile and a shrug.

"We in the military are quite often required to maintain secrecy," Captain Montgomery stated somewhat officiously.

"Oooh—like what?" Candide prodded lightly. Montgomery playfully shook a scolding finger at her and turned his attention to Poe.

"What about you, Mr. Poe? Did you ever serve in the military?"

"Only in a manner of speaking, and only briefly," Poe admitted, taking a sip of wine to dim the dryness in his throat. He noted that they all seemed inclined to speak of anything save the original question Reverend Farr had posed.

"I was actually accepted into the military academy at West Point and did quite well there in some respects."

"But?" Montgomery prompted.

"But I soon ended up being expelled from its hallowed halls due to a variety of…indiscretions."

"Do tell!" Candide urged.

"Best I not," Poe replied, chuckling softly. "Let us just say that I was a better scholar than I was a soldier."

Barely had he spoken when he was struck by a sudden, brief fit of coughing, which he mostly muffled with his napkin. To ease the spell, he took another sip of wine, finding it a bit difficult to swallow.

Perhaps surprisingly, Captain Montgomery seemed disinclined to judge Poe's military failure harshly.

"You may not have been entirely at fault, Mr. Poe. Not every man is cut out for the kind of life demanded by service in the military. I know this very well."

"I daresay it must have suited you, Captain Montgomery," Red Death offered. "You've even seen combat during your service, have you not?"

"I have," Montgomery confirmed, while he and the others at the table once again marveled at the personal knowledge of each of them that was possessed by their masked host. "In one of the campaigns in Florida against the Seminole Indians."

"Aaah!" Candide once more gushes in her best breathless voice. "What were they like, General? Those red savages, I mean."

"I'm only a captain, young lady," Montgomery corrected. "And believe me, when a man is pointing a weapon at you—be he savage or saint—your life is equally at risk."

"Yet you came through the travail," Reverend Farr said. "No doubt through the grace of God."

"No doubt," Montgomery replied somewhat curtly.

It was obvious he wished to speak no further of the matter, nor did Poe wonder at this. He had known other veterans who were reticent to speak of their war experiences.

"As always," Red Death eventually declared, "the dinner conversation has been both enlightening and entertaining." He rose from his chair.

"...at West Point and did quite well there in some respects."

"But other matters demand my attention."

What sort of matters might that be? Poe pondered.

Taking this as their own cue, the remaining contestants also made as if to quit the table, to be led away to their respective bedchambers.

"No, no," Red Death said, gesturing for them to remain seated. "Continue to enjoy your repast; I insist." With a swirl of his cape he then swept from the room, leaving the small group of contestants to their own devices.

"We've got to find a way to get out of here!" Reverend Farr exclaimed in a hushed but urgent voice, casting his eyes about to make sure they were not being spied upon.

"It seems clear to me now that this is no more than an elaborate scheme to *murder* the lot of us, one by one!"

"Our rather flamboyant host made no effort to hide from us the fact that our very lives would be the stakes for which we played in his Byzantine game," Poe said.

"The sort of 'game' wherein the loser forfeits his life hasn't been engaged in since the godless days of the depraved Roman Empire!" Reverend Farr practically roared in response, abandoning any effort at muffling his words.

"I thought the Romans had *lots* of gods!" Candide Swan interjected, smiling at the clergyman and batting her eyes ingenuously.

"Don't act so obtuse, madam," Farr scolded. "Now is not the time for such. You know perfectly well what I mean. Just because that red-masked madman fancies himself a modern day *Caligula* doesn't mean we have to be the victims of his insanity!"

"Yet you willingly agreed to participate in this game of death, Reverend," Captain Montgomery reminded him.

"At the time, it seemed the proper thing to do," Farr blustered. "Now, I am not so sure."

"And do you have a *plan* for escaping from the festivities?" Montgomery pressed.

"Well…no. Not yet. But surely together we can devise some means of achieving that."

"In for a penny, in for a pound," Poe declared with fatalistic acceptance.

"I know *exactly* why I entered this contest…and I mean to see it through to the very end. Its end…or my own."

"I'm with you, Mr. Poe," Candide said almost wistfully, reaching out to squeeze his hand gently.

"There's no one alive who would regret my passing…so why should I?"

"I'm sure that's not true, Candide," Poe assured her, raising her hand to his lips and kissing the back of it lightly.

The lady of leisure smiled, not because of the gallant gesture but because this was the first time any of the others had been bothered to actually call her by name.

"And I am equally sure it *is* true, Mr. Poe. But I thank you for your graciousness."

"You all talk as if we're already dead," Captain Montgomery said before draining yet another glass of wine.

"I, on the other hand, have no intention of dying. Not any time soon, at least. I fully intend to disappoint Mr. Death by *winning* this little competition."

"And I hope you do," Poe told him. "I hope we all do." He then turned his face toward Farr.

"What say you now, Reverend?"

Farr's shoulders slumped as in defeat. "What can I say? I may be able to win alone—but I can't escape alone." He sighed wearily.

"Whatever fate awaits—it seems we'll all face it as best we can."

The conversation ended abruptly when the various canine companions of the remaining contestants suddenly appeared to lead them from the banquet hall.

As soon as he was ushered into his own room, Poe locked the door, lighted a candle and performed a thoroughly inspection of all the dark places within: the corners, a bare closet, even under the bed. Lastly, he made sure the room's double windows were securely latched.

Even then he did not feel compelled to retire. Instead, he felt nervous, slightly agitated.

So he simply sat and stared at the leaping flames in the fireplace, seeking to slow the stampede of troubling thoughts that raced through his brain.

But no man is complete master of his mind. It goes where it pleases... and he is helpless to do aught but follow.

CHAPTER 28

With a loud, choking gasp, Reverend Sojourn Farr bolted upright in his bed.

He sat there, breathing in and out deeply. He didn't recall what frightening nightmare had possessed him, but it had felt almost as if he had been drowning.

Fully awake now, his heart rate quickly returned to normal, and he silently chastised himself for reacting so strongly to a mere dream. His right hand went to his face to wipe away the sweat he felt flowing from his forehead.

Oddly, it came away far wetter than one would expect from mere perspiration alone. He ran his fingers through his graying hair, and found that it too was soaked.

As was the front of his nightshirt. He feared he may have developed some sort of raging fever, but his brow was not warm to the touch.

He felt a sudden pressure on his chest, as if an unseen hand was pressing firmly against it. Such was the force it exerted that he fell back against the mattress.

It was not the feathery softness of the pillow his head struck, however—but water! With a loud splash he broke its surface, plunged beneath it,

Farr barely had time to suck in a short gasp of air before he found himself completely submerged in warm, murky water.

It was not particularly deep; Farr could feel the bottom of whatever body he found himself in with his kicking feet.

But the pressure bearing down on his chest remained constant, preventing him from coming up for air.

He tried to grab the hands, the arms that held him down, but found nothing of any real substance. Yet the weight holding him down was very real and constant.

As his insufficiently inflated lungs began to burn slightly, the pressure was removed and the same invisible hands that had held him under now seemed to be pulling him back up.

Like a great fish that had been hauled aboard a boat, Farr opened and closed his mouth rapidly as he rose above the water, inhaling blessed air.

As the droplets fell away from his eyes, he saw that he was no longer lying in his bed but rather outdoors in a narrow, shallow creek.

He cried out in horror as he saw an ominous figure standing over him, up to its waist in the water, holding him up by the front of his nightshirt. This figure looked like a dark and threatening image of some biblical patriarch. A wild mane of white hair blew in the wind; an equally silver, full beard hung down to his chest.

"Reverend Mordecai?" Farr gasped in disbelief.

He knew he could not be seeing what his stinging eyes told him he was seeing. The Reverend Mordecai Mayweather had passed away decades ago—not long after he had baptized a teenaged Sojourn Farr.

And indeed this intimidating figure was only a distortion of the true image of that holy man. Its skin was pallid, its eyes and cheeks deeply sunken. Its lips peeled back from teeth that were black with rot and it glared hatefully down at Farr.

Then this mockery of a minister again pushed Farr beneath the water.

Given a moment's more warning, Farr was able to draw in a deeper breath this time. Still, his struggles again proved useless and the pressure squeezing in on him from all sides threatened to crush his heaving chest.

Seconds before his lips would have been pushed open and he would have been forced to inhale water into his lungs, he found himself again pulled up out of the suffocating stream.

As he surfaced, sputtering and coughing, he heard voices singing. Twisting his head to one side, he saw a dozen other figures assembled on the banks of the creek. All were dressed in white robes and all had the look of freshly resurrected corpses.

From their dried and decayed vocal chords rose a croaking rendition of "Shall We Gather at the River?"

"You don't really want to be cleansed of your wickedness, do you, boy?" the desiccated version of Reverend Mayweather roared at him in his distinctive, stentorian voice.

"I do!" Farr cried. In his ears, his own voce sounded like that of the boy he had been on the day of his actual baptism.

"You lie!" the baptizer accused. "Your lips say the words—but your heart is full of sin. You don't want to be saved!"

"I do! I do! God help me—I do!"

"Then let the Holy Spirit in, boy—or else drown in your own wickedness!"

Farr felt himself being pushed under the stream yet again, so deeply that his entire body rested on its floor, his flailing limbs stirring up a cloud of mud and silt.

This time, it seemed as if the maniacal baptizer had no intention of ever pulling Farr back from the watery abyss. Farr's eyes were wide with fear and his lungs burned as if they were being baked from the inside. Desperate to escape the clutches of a watery death, he began to struggle more fiercely.

Had an uninvolved onlooker been watching Farr at this moment, he would have seen a man who, though seemingly lying alone in his bed, was lashing out wildly with fists and feet as if he was engaged in mortal combat with some invisible foe while gasping as if he was being denied air to breathe.

In his spiritually induced delusion, Farr felt his fingers gouging thin furrows in the muddy bottom of the stream in which he was perilously close to drowning.

In the reality of his bedchamber, his left arm shot out to one side and his hand fell atop a familiar object lying atop his nightstand.

It was his Bible.

His fingers slid across the pebbled surface of its well-worn cover, closing in around it. He lifted it without thinking and, as he had done on countless occasions, pulled it to him and clutched it to his breast.

In the instant that he did, the pressure holding him down in the dark depths of the stream was removed from his body. He shot to the surface, spewing water from his lungs and replacing it with saving oxygen. As it entered his heaving chest, even more dark water was expelled.

Hacking and coughing, he looked about him. The horrendous caricature of Reverend Mayweather was gone. The ghostly choir was gone.

The stream in which he had nearly drowned was gone.

He once more was fully aware that he was lying in his own bed, gasping and sobbing. His face was still moist, but this time it was only from fear-fraught perspiration.

Farr rolled off the bed, falling onto his knees beside it. Gripping the saving grace of his Bible in both hands now, he bowed his head and began to pray with all the fervor of his being.

He would eventually fall asleep while still on his knees.

CHAPTER 29

In yet another of the palace's seemingly endless number of bedchambers, Captain Albert Montgomery, aided as usual by the consumption of copious amounts of wine, slumbered deeply.

But the sound that now intruded on his consciousness was loud enough, persistent enough, to penetrate even a spirit-fueled stupor and awaken him.

Every muscle in his slender body grew taut as he soon came to recognize the source of the throbbing, monotonous beating. Though it had been several years since he had first and last heard it, it was a sound he could not, would not ever forget.

It was the ominous pounding of Indian *war drums*.

He tried at first to ignore the thrumming, but it grew so deeply loud as to vibrate the very bed in which he lay.

As he had done every night since he had foolishly and impulsively accepted Red Death's challenge, Montgomery had retired fully clothed, save for his boots. He sat up, swung his long legs over the side of the bed and stamped his feet into them.

He then went for his gun belt, hanging as usual from the bedpost so as to be close at hand, within easy reach. Buckling it around his waist, he made sure the pistol as his side slid smoothly in and out of its holster.

After lighting a candle, the soldier began a slow and methodical patrol around the confines of the bedchamber, hoping to find the source of the drumming. It seemed as if it came from nowhere—and from everywhere.

And it was growing louder.

The rhythm of it also become even more familiar to him, until he became certain that it was identical to the throbbing call to arms he had heard among the Seminole Indians against whom the U.S. Army had campaigned more than a decade-and-a-half earlier.

The impossibility of such an occurrence was irrelevant: every moment Montgomery had spent in this memorial to madness had been beyond his imagining.

Now, other noises began to intrude upon his consciousness, joining with the pulse of the drums. These, too, carried memories for Montgomery: the shrieks of exotic birds, the buzzing of mosquitoes so large and in such numbers that they threatened to drain a man's blood to the point of death.

Splashing water and a precipitous rise in humidity caused Montgomery to break into a heavy sweat. It felt reminiscent of the bouts of malaria that still on occasion plagued him: a memento of the days and nights he was forced to spend in the fetid swamplands the Seminoles called home.

Supplanting all the myriad other noises, a low, menacing growl sounded behind the soldier. Montgomery began a slow turnaround, his right hand creeping toward the butt of his pistol.

Less than a dozen feet away from him, wallowing in a shallow pool of stagnant water that now inexplicably covered the floor of the bedchamber, lay a darkly scaled *alligator*. Even in the muted lighting, Montgomery could see that the reptilian monster was itself a good ten feet in length from toothy snout to waving, armored tail.

With no further warning, the beast launched itself forward. Its jaws opened, revealing row upon row of long, jagged, yellowed teeth. Deceptively fast, given its enormity, the gator flashed toward Montgomery. It was a machine made of flesh, built for only one purpose.

To kill.

CHAPTER 30

Edgar Poe was abed, but sleep was proving to be elusive. Besides the turmoil now constantly churning in his brain, he was feeling slightly ill physically as well. The soreness in his throat had worsened somewhat, his discomfort compounded by an aching in his joints that he hoped was nothing more than a calling card left by his physical exertions of the last few days. The stiffness in his fingers he attributed directly to the scratches and gouges sustained by his struggles against the manic flock of birds the night before.

When a sound began to intrude upon his consciousness, he focused his attention on it. At first, he took it to be the steady beating of some distant drum.

As he listened closely, though, it seemed that the drumming was coming not from afar but from within his own room.

Thrum-thrum-thrum.

There was, he thought, only one thing that could explain the steady tone.

Thrum-thrum-thrum.

It was the sound of a human *heartbeat.*

THRUM-THRUM-THRUM.

Fear stirred within him as the sound of the throbbing heart grew louder. Given the unholy terrors he had already withstood in this house of wonder and horror, who knew what sort of monstrous beast now crouched hidden somewhere within the confines of his bedchamber?

His hand rose to his aching throat, his fingers happening to fall upon the artery that fed blood to the brain. Amazingly, he found that his pulse was pounding in exact time with the sound of the heartbeat he was hearing.

He felt rather foolish as he realized that he had been feeling rather than truly hearing his own heartbeat pounding in his ears. That realization alone caused the rapid beating to slow and grow less intense within his skull.

Poe chided himself as he swiped a sheen of sweat from his forehead.

"Stop reading your own stories," he said softly. "The only monster in this room—is yourself."

He rolled onto his left side, determined to will himself to sleep.

There would be no such wishing away of the horror being witnessed at that same moment by Captain Montgomery.

With the speed of a galloping pony, the ravenous alligator rapidly closed the distance between itself and its prey.

Montgomery frantically tugged at the butt of his pistol, felt the weapon nearly fly away from his fingers before he tightened his grip.

So close was the attacking reptile now that there was neither time nor need to take careful aim.

As quickly as he was able, Montgomery cocked and fired the cap and ball pistol, sending leaden projectiles screaming straight into the gaping maw of the alligator.

Literally staring into the face of death, the soldier screamed and threw his arms in front of his face, falling over backwards into the shallow water.

He was more amazed than relieved when he did not feel reptilian teeth close on his body or rip his flesh.

He slowly opened his eyes; of the gator there was now no sign that it had ever been there.

He was still lying in a pool of stagnant water, but strangely, seemed to no longer be inside his bedchamber. Instead, the setting seemed to have now completely transformed into the steaming everglades he had quickly come to despise during the Army's campaign against the Seminoles.

The sounds of wildlife were even more pervasive. Thick strands of Spanish moss hung nearly to the waterline from trees that grew so close together that they nearly formed a solid roof over the swamp.

The air he breathed was so heavy with moisture as to be almost tangible. In the heat and humidity, Montgomery was perspiring even more heavily by the time all this had registered on his brain.

He gasped fearfully as he then did again see the alligator that had attacked him—relaxing only slightly as he realized the creature was dead, its corpse slowly floating away from him on some slight and unseen current.

"Mighty fine shootin', Lieutenant," a raspy voice said from nearby. The declaration ended in a cackling laugh.

"Yessir—mighty fine!"

At the sound of this disturbingly familiar voice, Montgomery scrambled to his feet. The few and heavily filtered rays of moonlight coming from above provided just enough illumination for him to make out the figure of another man, standing sideways to him and several feet away.

This man, like Montgomery himself, was dressed in military uniform. His, however, was caked with filth and torn in several places. On the sleeve of his tunic could be seen the insignia of a noncommissioned officer in the U.S. Infantry.

"Is that you, Sergeant Bellows?" Montgomery asked in a voice that cracked like that of a pubescent boy.

"It is, Lieutenant," the gaunt and shadowy figure replied. His voice was solid, though laced with weariness.

"I'm kinda surprised you remember me."

"No," Montgomery muttered in disbelief. "No, no, no, no, no. It can't be you. You're dead!"

"That be true, right enough," the ghostly soldier confirmed. Ever so slowly, he turned to look directly at his former commanding officer.

A groan from deep within spilled out of Montgomery's mouth as the side of the specter's face that had been hidden from his sight now came into full view.

The ghostly sergeant's right eye and upper jaw were missing, as if sheared away by a battle-ax—as was a portion of his scalp!

CHAPTER 31

Candide Swan felt equal parts frightened and flattered when she was ushered into her bedchamber that evening.

It was well lit, with several candles suffusing it with a soft glow that in other times and places would have offered a comforting welcome.

In *this* time and place, though, they aroused her already innately suspicious nature (a trait she would have been irked to learn she shared with the highwayman Edward Carp).

"What's with all the candles?" she asked her attendant, one of the odd little dog men who led them all about. This one's poodle-like head canted slightly to one side before it answered.

"I was instructed to light them, mistress," he replied in an only slightly obsequious tone of voice. "We thought it would give the room more of a sense of warmth."

Candide stared rather harshly at the dog man for a moment. His large, expressive eyes, set against the tight, white curls of his furry face, seemed to hold neither guile nor deceit. Candide's own features at last softened.

"How thoughtful," she said, smiling at the pooch. Leaning down, she softly scratched a spot under his chin.

"You're such a good boy," she told him sweetly, giving the dog man a light kiss on the tip of his snout.

"Thank you, ma'am," he said awkwardly. Candide wondered if he might be blushing somewhere underneath all that luxuriant fur.

"I'll see you in the morning," he said by way of farewell.

"I hope."

Candide scowled at that last line. "I assure you, little man—you will!" she huffed before rather abruptly closing the door in his startled face.

Turning, she examined the layout of her room. In most respects it was virtually identical to the others in which she had spent the previous nights, with one small but quickly noticeable exception.

Mirrors.

Every room in which she had slept had a mirror on one wall. The walls of this room, however, all sported multiple looking glasses.

Candide had to admit to herself that this touch was a pleasing one. It had been her alluring good looks that raised her out of her humble origins and she took great pride in them. Seeing them reflected back at her was a source of both satisfaction and joy.

She stepped over to the one nearest to her, conveniently placed at eye level above the room's wash basin. Given the chamber's bright lighting, she was able to see her reflected image with total clarity.

She turned her head slightly from side to side, though her eyes never left the reflection. She smiled upon seeing that, as always, her hair was as close to being perfectly coifed as could be expected given her current situation.

She then leaned in closer for the most important inspection, so close that her face was mere inches away from the mirror's pristine, polished surface.

This lady of leisure tilted her head back slightly, running expert fingers over the taut skin of her neck, feeling for and finding no imperfections in its tone. She leaned still closer to the mirror.

She frowned slightly. Was that a previously unseen line at the outer corner of her right eye? She dabbed at it lightly with one finger, the smile returning to her lips when she saw it was only an illusion of the lighting, one quickly dispelled by smoothing the powder that helped conceal any imperfections that might threaten to make their presence known.

Next, she examined the corners of her full lips, happily finding them to be unmarred save for the natural curves at either side that were almost but not quite dimples. Puckering those lips, she blew a kiss to her reflection.

Nor was it purely vanity that fueled this nightly ritual of hers. Experience had taught her what became of women of her ilk when age began to take its inevitable toll.

Having seen more than one aged doyenne reduced to hustling for drinks in disreputable bars when their looks had faded and they no longer stirred desire in men so readily, Candide had always striven to save and invest the bulk of her earnings wisely against that day when she, too, would inescapably find she no longer fanned the flames of lust in the bellies of male admirers.

Having assured (possibly deluded) herself that she was still a fully desirable woman, Candide leaned down over the basin and gently cleansed her face. "Washing away the cares of the day," was how she referred to it.

A thick, soft towel had also been provided and she lifted it to her face, lightly dabbing it to absorb the wetness. Setting the towel back down, she again looked at her reflection in the mirror.

And saw a monster looking back at her!

The beastly image glaring at her would be called that of a woman only by the most generous of observers. White hair with the brittle texture of dry straw sat atop its head like some wildly tangled bird's nest.

This mess framed a face of witchly proportions. One eye was nearly closed, while the other bulged hideously from its socket. It was an unhealthy yellow in color; some sort of viscous fluid seeped from its inner corner.

Its nose was long and hooked, its face and neck scored with wrinkles resembling a network of crevices on some bleak and lifeless lunar landscape.

The creature in the mirror appeared to be smiling, its leer revealing rows of brown and uneven teeth, punctuated by occasional black gaps where there were no teeth at all.

Candide cried out in horror and disgust and her feet pedaled her backwards away from the monstrous old crone. She scarce noticed that she had covered the width of the room until she slammed painfully into the opposite wall.

Wincing, she spun to find herself gazing into yet another of the myriad mirrors hanging on the walls—and into yet another frightful face.

Once more, it was the image of an old woman she saw there. There were slight differences in its appearance, though. One eye drooped awkwardly, dragged down by scar tissue that ran down from its outer corner to below the line of her jaw—indicative of an old wound made by the blade of either knife or razor.

Candide recoiled, only to come face-to-face with yet another mirrored image of yet another aged and worn woman. This one had the glazed eyes and blank stare of the habitual inhabitant of an opium parlor. Drool slid unheeded down her chin.

Now repulsed more than frightened by these views of womanhood gone to seed, Candide slid away along the wall until she faced another, larger mirror. Resigned to what it would present to her, she gazed into its glassy surface.

Due to its size, this mirror contained the image of not just a woman's face but her entire upper body. She was old, just as the others had been, but seemed to be asleep or unconscious, with her eyes tightly closed.

Or perhaps she was dead, Candide thought. The woman's worn and wrinkled face certainly exhibited the effects of either long or hard years, possibly both.

As with the other reflections, Candide found this image to be repugnant. Yet there was something about it that also piqued her curiosity, seeming to have more emotional depth to it than had they.

As if compelled, Candide leaned closer to the mirror, examining the image there more intently. Her vision traced over every line of the slumbering old woman's face.

With suddenness, she realized what about this woman had drawn her in rather than repelled her away.

The face in the mirror greatly and disturbingly resembled Candide's, though grown old and indescribably tired. That simple realization horrified Candide more than had any of the other haggard and ugly images.

She cried out as the eyes of the old woman in the mirror unexpectedly snapped open.

Though red and rheumy, they were eyes that seemed capable of boring straight into Candide's heart—where they would doubtless gaze upon nothing but a dark and empty chasm.

"Oh, Lord," Candide moaned, pulling back away from the mirror.

She did not move quickly enough—for a pair of bony, gnarled hands flew forward from the looking glass, seizing her by the throat.

Candide's first thought was that the crone intended to drag her into the mirror alongside her. But as the fingers encircling her neck closed on her flesh with inhuman strength that belied their decrepit appearance, she realized the wraith's real intention was to choke the very life from her body.

Finding herself unable to pull free of the murderous manifestation's grip, Candide began to frantically claw at its skeletal arms.

To her dismay, she saw strips of its flesh literally tear away beneath her nails, exposing the tissue and even bone that lay below the skin. No blood escaped from these lacerations, but only a smell of decomposition.

Gasping from both the odor and the lack of air reaching her lungs, Candide's hands fell away from the wraith and began to flail about madly.

Pain in her fingertips as they momentarily flashed through the flames of one of the nearby candles barely registered on Candide's brain, which was fogging over from the loss of oxygen. Her tongue hung limply from her mouth and her eyes began to roll to the top of her head.

Her right hand flung itself toward the candle again, striking it and toppling it and its heavy silver holder over. One desperate thought other than those of impending death managed to worm its way to the surface of her consciousness and she wrapped her fingers around the fallen candlestick.

With what little strength still lingered in her body, she swung the candlestick—not at the arms of the creature that was murdering her, but at the surface of the mirror from which those appendages extended.

She was rewarded with the crunching sound of cracks appearing in the glass. She swung the candlestick again and a web of fissures spread across the mirror. At the same time, the grasp of the bony fingers wrapped around her throat loosened: only slightly, but enough for a little air to again race down into her nearly collapsed lungs.

Strengthened and encouraged, Candide swung the candlestick with even greater force. She thought she heard the harridan in the mirror scream, but the sound she detected may have been nothing more than that of breaking glass.

One more frenzied blow and the mirror shattered into hundreds of sparkling shards. As it did, the ghostly hands strangling Candide became as immaterial as smoke before vanishing altogether.

With a retching sound, Candide slid down the wall and fell limply on the floor. Her free hand stroked her inflamed throat as she loudly sucked in reviving air.

She raised her right hand, looking with relief at the candlestick still clutched in its grip. At the sight of a dark, wet stain on its base, she brought it closer to her face, flinching and groaning at what she saw.

Unlike her nails where she had clawed at the wraith's arms, the candlestick was spattered with *blood*.

And it was not her own.

Short, wheezing gasps of air came from Candide's mouth as she pushed herself up from the floor, using the wall for support. With eyes partially closed, she glanced sideways to locate the nearest of the remaining mirrors—then practically hurled herself at it.

Holding the candlestick firmly in both hands, she slammed its solid base into that mirror.

As it shattered, tiny slivers of flying glass nicked her hands, but for once she paid no heed to anything that might blemish her physically.

More disturbing was the howls of pain that now distinctly issued from within the depths of the looking glass as it splintered. But Candide was unmindful of this as well—and to the chorus of similar agonized shrieks she continued to elicit as she made a complete circuit of the chamber smashing every mirror on its walls.

Nor were her labors completed when the last of them lay in impotent shards at her feet. She made a second round of the room, extinguishing every candle that she may not be able to see so much as a tiny fragment of her own reflection in the pieces of mirror littering the floor.

She would have extinguished even the flames of the fireplace and thus plunged the room into complete and total darkness, save for the fact that she needed the warmth it provided against the chill of the night and the shivering cold in her soul.

Instead, she pulled the top coverlet from her bed and crawled into the chair nearest to the fire.

Curling into a tight ball and pulling the cover completely over her, head and all…the woman at last cried herself to sleep.

CHAPTER 32

In another bedchamber, Edgar Poe had finally managed to doze off—only to be stirred awake by a fresh sound.

He felt anxious and on edge. His brow seemed flushed with slight fever and he thought that perhaps it was this and nothing more that had stirred him from his slumber.

But once fully awake he realized the sound was very real and continuing. And as before, it seemed to be originating on the other side of the chamber's windows.

Surely not black birds again?

No, for this noise was noticeably different.

Lighting the candle that sat atop his nightstand, Poe slid from the bed and cautiously padded to the other side of the room.

As he approached the closed windows, he became more convinced that the noise was not coming from birds, for it was not the pecking of beaks or the scratching of talons on the sill.

Yet there was a familiarity to it; it reminded him of the sound made by sand flowing relentlessly from the top of an hourglass to the bottom.

Drawing closer still, he could detect no shadowy forms flitting across the glass that might be cast by anything lurking beyond the leaded glass. Of course, regardless of its origin, he had no intention of repeating his mistake of the previous evening by opening the latch.

Yet then there was a movement, near the bottom of where the two windows met: just enough to catch his eye. He bent down, lowering the candle closer to facilitate his sight.

He was not frightened, but merely puzzled by what came into view. It appeared to be a thin stream of *dirt*, trickling through the almost imperceptible seam where the two panes of the window came together.

At that same moment, elsewhere in the manse, Captain Montgomery was nearly overwhelmed by the sights and sounds of the swamp that incredibly seemed to surround him now.

And by the *smells*.

He realized with a gut-wrenching spasm that some of the odor he detected was wafting toward him from the rotting though animated corpse of Sgt. Bellows. The poor man was as…ripe and pungent as was the wet and moldy foliage.

Combined, the sights, sounds and odors sparked suppressed sense memories within Montgomery, causing them to carry him flying back in time.

It could be said that the events he sought to erase with drink had begun with the onset of what came to be called the Second Seminole War: a conflict that began in 1835 and ran sporadically for nearly seven years.

This war of attrition had been sparked by the U.S. government's determined efforts to force the native Seminole Indians to leave their ancestral homes in Florida altogether and agree to be relocated to the designated Indian Territory a thousand miles away. Their removal, by force if necessary, had been authorized by act of Congress in the Indian Removal Act of 1830, the same infamous decree that would result in the deaths of thousands of Cherokee Indians along the hideous *Trail of Tears*.

On December 28, 1835, a force of 110 American soldiers under the command of Major Francis Dade was ambushed by a Seminole war party led by Chief Alligator. Only two badly wounded members of that ill-fated command survived the battle and were able to return to their base at Fort Brooke with the grim news.

This total military disaster was little noted by the American public then or later, for the word of it was far overshadowed by the stunning news that swept over the nation's collective consciousness less than three months af-

...the odor he detected was the rotting corpse of Sgt. Bellows.

ter the military debacle in Florida.

This was a story that came out of a revolutionary struggle in the northern Mexican province of Texas and dealt with the deaths of nearly 200 men in a battle that took place in a rundown former mission known to the locals as the *Alamo*.

Among the brave rebels who died together on the final day of that siege were James Bowie and David Crockett—men of renown whose fame grew even greater with their deaths.

But those who considered themselves to be brothers in arms with the soldiers who had lost their lives in the fetid swamps of Florida did not forget them or their sacrifice.

So it was that in February of 1836 a force led by Major Ethan Allen Hitchcock returned to the Everglades, searching for and finding what remained of the bodies of their fallen comrades. That was the totality of their mission, and upon burying the dead they immediately reversed course for the march back to Fort Brooke.

When scouts brought word that a party of Seminoles was on their tails, coming up fast behind them, Major Hitchcock tasked young Lieutenant Albert Montgomery with the job of remaining behind with fifteen men as a rear guard while the main body put safe distance between the two forces.

It was the prudent move for the commander to make, for the Seminole war party was no more than an hour behind the retreating column of soldiers. By the time they reached the rear guard, Lt. Montgomery had deployed all his men to good defensive positions, along with orders to maintain those positions until and unless ordered to abandon them.

The attack did not come immediately; the natives took time to send out their own scouts and devise their own strategy. This was fine with Montgomery; every minute's delay brought the rest of the command closer to the relative safety of Fort Brooke.

He was excited at the thought of what would be his first action, yet also slightly dismayed to see a faint tremor in his hands, feel a dryness in his throat that contrasted with the wet beads of perspiration that broke out on his forehead. If he didn't know better, he might think he was afraid, but such surely could not be. He sought to dismiss the very idea; he was from a family of soldiers, for whom valor was a given attribute.

When the attack finally did come, it was signaled by a long, loud and keening war cry. Then the Indians came charging forward out of the swamp like a dusky tidal wave.

Faced with this first true taste of combat, young Lt. Montgomery fully intended to be brave, to be stalwart.

When the reality of war came rushing toward him, however—he proved to be neither.

As the attacking warriors drew closer, Sgt. Bellows looked anxiously at his commanding officer. To his concern, he saw that Montgomery seemed frozen in place; he had not even drawn his own weapon.

"Give the order to open fire, sir!" the noncom hissed, loudly enough for the lieutenant but not the other soldiers to hear.

That should have been a simple enough thing to do: even Montgomery himself thought so. Yet no such order issued from his parched throat. His vocal chords seemed to be as paralyzed as did his other muscles.

"*Fire!*" Sgt. Bellows shouted at the top of his lungs.

Even at that, the volley of rifle fire that followed seemed to take the young officer by surprise, causing him to start.

Several Indians staggered and fell to the withering fire. The charge broke and their brothers retreated, carrying their dead and wounded with them.

"Reload!" Sgt. Bellows ordered his men. He again looked to Lt. Montgomery, only to see the young officer staring down in petrified horror at the body of a trooper who had taken a musket ball to the head. The dead soldier's eyes were still partially opened, and Montgomery felt certain they were staring at him in an accusatory fashion.

Montgomery's head slowly swiveled and he looked at Sgt. Bellows in a manner that silently pled for guidance. All he got in return was a look of disgust from the noncom.

Then came the yipping yell that signaled a fresh attack from the Seminoles. They were more spread out this time as they splashed forward through the shallow water.

This time, Sgt. Bellows did not wait for his commanding officer to issue any orders.

"Fire at will!" he shouted. "Make every shot count, boys!"

The sounds of gunfire from both sides of the battle were nearly deafening—yet amazingly not so loud as to drown out the terrible screams of the grievously wounded. So thick was the haze of black powder expelled from the guns that the combatants were often firing blindly.

Lt. Montgomery was at first unaware that he had begun to stiffly step backwards, his resolve starting to crack like fragile china. When he nearly tripped over the sprawled body of yet another fallen soldier, Montgomery's tenuous grip on courage completely shattered.

He didn't order his men to retreat, and thus lost all claim to honor. He simply turned and ran, giving no thought at all to saving any life but his own.

He had not gone far when a ragged voice shouting his name brought him to a skidding halt. He looked back to see Sgt. Bellows, kneeling beside the lifeless body of yet another slain soldier.

For a moment that seemed to stretch into eternity, the officer and the noncom gazed intently at each other. To his everlasting shame, Montgomery saw in Bellows' eyes none of the fear that so possessed him.

What he did see was anger and judgment: both directed at him.

Sgt. Bellows turned away at the war cry of an onrushing Seminole, firing his pistol at the warrior.

At the same time, Lt. Montgomery turned and resumed fleeing.

He did not run so fast or so far, though, that he could not still hear the gunfire in the distance behind him, coming both at and from the small band of Americans he had abandoned to their fate. The explosive sounds grew fainter and more sporadic before ceasing altogether.

Nor, once he had reached safety behind the stockade walls of Fort Brooke, did any sense of personal responsibility prevent him from inventing a false narrative of how he and his men together had repulsed the Indian war party at the cost of all lives save his own.

For this act of "bravery," Albert Montgomery had received medals and a battlefield promotion to captain. He was ashamed to accept either—but not to the point of refusing the honors.

"But how is it yer only a *captain*, now?" the ghostly image of Sgt. Bellows asked him pointedly, noting the insignia on Montgomery's tunic.

"I'd think by now you'd be at least a major, maybe even a colonel."

Montgomery tried to shrug away the implied criticism. "After things settled down with the Seminoles, there weren't many opportunities for an officer to advance on the battlefield. Not till we got into a shooting war with Mexico a decade later."

"What'd we fight *them* for?" the ghost quizzed.

"The usual reasons, I guess, Sergeant."

"So, why didn't you get promoted then?"

"I really see no reason to explain myself to you, Bellows."

The specter chuckled. "Then don't. Makes me no never mind."

Yet Montgomery did go on. "By that time, I'd gotten myself firmly ensconced where I always wanted to be—behind a nice, safe desk in Washington.

"Oh, I was offered the opportunity to accept a command in active duty out west if I wanted it."

"But you didn't want it."

"No," Montgomery replied bitterly. "I didn't want it."

"Once a coward, always a coward, eh, boyo?" Bellows said wickedly.

"I was going for help that day," Montgomery said weakly, still seeking to justify his perfidy.

"I believed that, with you directing them, the others would be able to hold off the Seminoles until I could return with reinforcements."

"That's a *lie*," another, previously unheard voice accused.

From out of the surrounding darkness, a second ghostly soldier emerged to stand beside Sgt. Bellows. He, too, bore the marks of having been scalped. Two feathered arrows protruded from his chest.

"Private Collins," Montgomery gasped.

"I'm surprised you remember my name," the specter said. "You never bothered to really get to know the men under your command."

"It's best that an officer not fraternize with the enlisted men," Montgomery said stiffly, as if reciting some section from a book of rules and regulations.

"Still," the specter said. "You knew I was the fastest runner in the whole platoon. Everybody knew it.

"You could have sent *me* runnin' to fetch help—but you didn't."

"It was already too late," Montgomery practically whimpered. "There was no need for *all* of us to die!"

"But all of us *did* die, Lieutenant," yet a third voice sang out.

"All but *you*."

From the concealment of haze, hanging moss, swarming insects and darkness, more figures emerged to assemble on either side of Sgt. Bellows. There were now fifteen specters in all.

All of them had been members of the cursed command led by then Lieutenant Montgomery. All of them had desperately fought and died while he had saved his own life by fleeing. All of them still bore the signs of their doomed last stand: bullet holes, pieces of cut and torn scalps, slashed throats, jagged rips from tomahawks and protruding arrows.

Montgomery's proper sensibilities swirled as he realized that most of them were naked as well. They had been stripped of their uniforms and their bodies mutilated in unspeakable manners by the victorious Seminoles.

And all of them now began to march slowly, ominously toward the officer who had abandoned them to their grisly fates.

CHAPTER 33

The trickle of dirt forcing its way through the bottom crack of Edgar Poe's windows had by now become a small stream, beginning to form in a pile on the floor below.

Then, with no more warning than a sudden, violent crash, it became a torrent that flung the windows open with such force that Poe was swept backwards off his feet.

He landed so hard that the back of his head bounced off the hardwood floor, momentarily knocking him senseless.

He seemingly regained his faculties in short order, only to find he was completely in the dark. For an instant he feared the blow to his head had rendered him blind.

He was having difficulty breathing as well—and realized with panicked terror that both were due to the fact that the influx of dirt now completely covered his face and was seeking to insinuate itself into both his nose and mouth.

That realization triggered a primordial despair within him that Poe shared with many people of his day.

The fear of *premature burial*!

Had his full senses been about him, he might have reasoned that *viviseputure*, as this phobia was technically termed, had at least a modicum of factual basis behind it. More than one body of a presumably dead individual had been exhumed or otherwise uncovered to find undeniable signs that the poor victim had been interred before true death had descended—only to then expire from lack of oxygen while frantically attempting to claw his or her way out of the grave.

The very thought of such a fate, one upon which he had often contemplated in the darkest hours of his frequent depressions, was enough to trigger now a severe panic attack within Poe's bosom.

With a surge of adrenaline-fueled strength, he lurched upward to a sitting position, gasping loudly and deeply as he sucked blessed air into his burning lungs.

As he willed his breath and heart rate to a semblance of normal, he realized that he was still cloaked in virtual darkness.

The cascading dirt, now at nearly knee-high depth throughout the room, had smothered the flames within his fireplace and hence its light.

The candle Poe had carried with him to the windows had been dislodged from his hand and extinguished. The only light within the chamber was the pale glow cast by a candle that at the moment perched above the rising tide of dirt upon his nightstand.

It was enough illumination for him to see that the torrent of smothering soil was continuing to flow in unabated through the open windows.

Which left only the locked door of the bedchamber as a possible means of egress.

There had seemed to be no slightest hint of prevarication when Red Death had solemnly warned all the contestants that to open their doors at night would be to invite in their own doom.

But in the moment, the fear of some unknown and undefined danger lurking without was to Poe secondary to the very real and immediate threat posed by the rising tide of earth.

There was no time to waste; the dirt was almost exactly at the level of his knees. Poe could barely raise his feet from the floor, relying on the strength in his screaming leg muscles to propel him forward.

Even upon reaching the portal, though, Poe hesitated. Every instinct he had told him that certain death awaited him on the other side of the door—just as it did on this side.

He flipped the latch on the lock and pulled on the knob.

Nothing happened.

It was too late. So high had the level of dirt risen that its sheer weight made it impossible for Poe alone to open the heavy door. And the level was continuing to rise.

"Help me!" Poe shouted frantically, pounding on the door with one fist while continuing to tug in vain on the knob with the other hand. Yet even as he did so, he knew in his heart no help would be coming.

After all, who was there that might even hear his entreaties—the mean-spirited Reynolds?

The dirt was now above his knees.

CHAPTER 34

As the ghosts of dead soldiers shambled closer to him, Captain Montgomery now noticed that in addition to their various wounds and deliberately inflicted mutilations, their bodies also showed signs of decomposition.

Unlike with their earlier, ill-fated comrades, no effort had even been made to recover and bury their remains; higher authorities had deemed it too high a risk for such a small contingent.

Though the rational part of his brain told Montgomery that these specters were just that—unreal in any physical sense of the term—his eyes told him otherwise.

As did his sense of smell. The stench of putrefaction—far stronger than that given off earlier by Sgt. Bellows' corpse alone—swept over him so strongly that his belly rebelled against him. His body bent over double as it emptied itself of all its contents: mostly wine.

"What right did you have to buy your life at the cost of ours?" one of the spectral soldiers demanded to know.

"I'm sorry," Montgomery whispered in a hoarse voice, his throat burning from the acidic residue of his own vomit.

"Not as sorry as yer gonna be!" the ghostly doppelganger of Sgt. Bellows warned ominously.

As if following an unspoken command, the dead soldiers fanned out to stand shoulder to shoulder. They then began to slowly march in lockstep toward Montgomery.

"Don't come any closer," the captain ordered in a voice that trembled too much to carry any air of true authority. He raised his pistol threateningly. "I'll shoot!"

The spectral soldiers halted their advance, exchanging puzzled glances back and forth. They next burst into howls of unholy laughter.

"And just how much damage do you think a slug can *do* to someone who's already dead, Lieutenant?" Sgt. Bellows asked rhetorically.

Before Montgomery could reply or even think of a reply, a blood-curdling scream shattered the heavy night air. It came not from the ghostly soldiers, though, but from somewhere beyond them.

Splashing water spoke of advancing bodies, figures that now burst from the cover of the trees and into plain sight.

To his even greater dismay, Montgomery realized it was a Seminole war party, charging straight toward him!

"Form a skirmish line!" the frightened officer shouted, instinct bringing the order to his tongue.

"And do *what*, Lieutenant sir?" the spectral Sgt. Bellows replied. He held both hands forward, empty palms out.

"After they'd had all their *fun* with us—them heathen devils took our weapons!"

Bellows' ghost motioned to his fellow phantoms. "What say, boys? Let's see if an officer and a gentleman fares any better than us lowly foot soldiers did."

In unspoken agreement, the line of soldiers parted ranks, leaving the way clear for the attackers. The charging Indians paid them no mind, sweeping past them and heading straight for Montgomery.

The disgraced officer pulled the trigger on his pistol, but the resulting shot found no target. When he cocked the hammer and tugged on the trigger a second time, nothing happened; he had expended all the other live shells earlier on the attacking alligator.

There was no time to do anything else. The foremost of the raging Seminoles slammed into him. Many hands clutched at him, dragging him to the soggy ground and holding him in a viselike grip.

Even above their triumphant cries in his ears, Montgomery could hear Sgt. Bellows and the other soldiers howling with glee over his plight.

And finally, as a razor sharp knife blade was being drawn agonizingly across his hairline, Captain Albert Montgomery learned one final, awful truth.

It was not necessary for a man to be *dead* yet in order for him to be *scalped*!

CHAPTER 35

Edgar Poe might have been able to hear Captain Montgomery's final series of shrieks through the walls of his bedchamber—had not his ears been completely filled by the sounds of the onrushing dirt and his own fearful gasps.

To his racing mind it appeared that he was trapped beyond all hope. The chamber door could not be opened and the windows were the source of the unceasing flood of soil. And these were the only possible means of escape.

Or were they?

There was still the fireplace, he realized, now growing cold. More specifically, there was the chimney leading up from the fireplace and which just might be wide enough to present a way up and out.

If he could reach it.

For all his extant athleticism, Poe quickly realized that wading through the accumulating dirt was extremely difficult: like trying to walk through densely packed, high snow drifts. At times he found it necessary to grab his legs by both hands, literally pulling them forward.

His foot struck one corner of a small ottoman hidden from view beneath the rising soil. His balance upset, he pitched forward. Once again he found himself completely submerged in the clawing grip of the grave.

As before, he nearly panicked with unreasoning terror. It took all the power of his self-control to keep from screaming in fear and thus opening his mouth to a deluge of dirt that would have most certainly choked him to death.

It was not self-preservation alone, but a renewed sense of his purpose for being here that motivated him to hunch his shoulders and push himself upward.

His first effort was in vain and he now felt the weight of the soil pressing against him from all sides. That pressure threatened to squeeze the last precious breath from his lungs, which would in turn cause him to inhale involuntarily and suck soil into airways that would then collapse.

Body quivering as if from intense cold, he pushed upward once more. This time, his head at last broke the surface of his grainy bonds. He desperately inhaled before falling back under the sod.

The fresh air that now filled his lungs renewed his strength. He doubled his efforts and in a spray of dirt he broke loose and again rose to his feet.

The flowing dirt had not yet risen high enough to extinguish the lonesome candle perched atop his nightstand, so Poe could still see to make his way, albeit painfully slowly, toward the beckoning maw of the fireplace.

He gasped in despair when at last he reached it only to find that it was rapidly filling with the suffocating soil.

Like a mole gone mad he began to furiously burrow at it with both hands, sending clods of dirt flying back behind him. When he had disposed of enough of it, he dived into the fireplace and thrust his head and shoulders into its flue.

The chimney rising upward from the pit's belly was barely wider than his own slender body, while its brick sides offered almost no purchase by which he might attempt to climb up within it. And the dirt was continuing its inexorable rise below him.

His only option was to press his back against one side of the chimney and his hands and knees against the other, maintaining constant pressure outward while simultaneously pushing himself upward.

The confined space went totally black; the tide of dirt had at last reached and snuffed out the bedchamber's only remaining candle. Tilting his head back as far as the confined space would allow, Poe attempted to discern the distance he would have to assay to climb in order to reach the top of the chimney.

All he saw above him was an empty void.

A pressure against the soles of his feet told him the dirt was following him up the chimney and that drove all thoughts from his mind save those needed to concentrate on pushing himself ever upward. He clawed at any slight indentation between the bricks in the chimney, frantically inching his way higher even as the column of dirt pursued him from below.

His arms and legs began to quiver, then shake uncontrollably, and he knew his waning strength would fail him long before he could reach the top of the chimney. Like the interminable hallways he trod each day, the opening at the top of the flue seemed to be miles away.

Poe paused in his efforts, restoring spent muscles and regaining ragged breath. As his breathing slowed, he came to realize that his own panting was the only sound he was hearing.

The rumbling of the flood of dirt had ceased, as if its source had stopped its movement upward.

Even as that realization dawned upon him, though, the strength in his cramping arms and legs gave way. With a fearful cry, he plummeted downward.

A loud gasp issued from his lips as he landed atop the ominous column of soil. This time, however, the dirt did not swallow him but simply acted to cushion his fall.

Moments later, he did experience a decided sinking sensation—but he was not falling *into* the grasp of the dirt but rather falling along with it.

Like water after a flash flood, the dirt inside the chimney rapidly descended, carrying Poe along with it.

By the time he tumbled wildly down the chimney, out of the fireplace and onto the floor of his bedchamber, there was just enough starlight filtering in through the open windows for him to see that the entire blanket of dirt was retreating—like a river impossibly flowing backwards.

His heart still pumping furiously, Poe staggered across the room and slammed the twin windows closed. There was an empty wardrobe nearby and with much straining he was able to drag it over and tilt it in a manner whereby the pressure of its weight against the windows would likely hold them closed.

Even this precaution did not put his strained mind at ease. He righted a chair, brushed it free of remnants of dirt as best he could, pushed it to a spot next to the chamber door and dropped heavily down into its cushioned seat.

It was his plan to spend the rest of the night there and attempt to avail himself of at least intermittent sleep. If the flood of dirt was to make a return appearance, he should easily hear it in time to take his chances on flinging open the door and exiting from the room.

As Poe brushed dirt from his increasingly soiled clothing with the back of one hand, he even managed to produce a light, dark chuckle.

"Even in the grave, all is not lost," he muttered softly as he closed his red-rimmed eyes.

CHAPTER 36

The following morning, as had become the usual ritual, the pugnacious and pompous little dog man Reynolds marched briskly up to the door of his assigned charge's bedchamber and commenced his series of increasing knocks.

"Still alive?" he said once again after the sequence of three knocks. Even his virtually featureless face clearly showed his disappointment as the bedraggled Edgar Poe flung open his portal.

"Too bad."

What would have been an eyebrow on a man's face arched upward as Reynolds studied the writer. Poe realized he must have presented quite an ungainly sight.

As proof, if by now any such was needed, of the reality of the terrifying events of the previous evening, upon awakening Poe had found that the water remaining in the pitcher at his bedside (which miraculously had remained both upright and unbroken) was too muddied to be used in his usual morning ablutions.

He had removed the covers from his bed and employed the relatively clean sheet beneath to clean his hands and face as best he could. The same with his clothing which, in addition to the filth, had also sustained a few new tears in the strained fabric.

As he stoically commenced that day's march, he found himself to be more physically ill as well; his enervation doubtless exacerbated by his increasing lack of sleep.

He found that the evenly placed flagons of water in the hallway down which he traveled held little appeal to him, save for when he used the bulk of the contents of the first such to more thoroughly wash himself free of the remaining stains of dirt.

Poe sought to take at least faint heart in the fact that he could now clearly tell that there was greater distance behind him than there appeared to be ahead of him in the otherwise seemingly endless corridor down which he was determined to keep trekking.

His battered but still functioning pocket watch told him they were near-ing the end of the day when there occurred an unexpected variation to the normal routine. Another of the palace's dog manservants, its head resem-bling that of a terrier, suddenly appeared as if from the ether. After urging Reynolds to join him a short distance away, the two humanesque canines entered into s hushed but spirited conversation.

Based on the occasional furtive glances they cast in his direction, Poe assumed they were talking about him. Such was his physical condition that he didn't much care; his every joint was aching and he once again felt fever-ish, so the respite this intrusion provided was welcomed. He sagged against the wall, resting his weight against its solidity.

Finally, Reynolds broke off his quiet but intense conversation with the other dog man with a curt nod of his bullet head. He strolled back toward Poe, as usual licking at his foamy lips.

"You stink," the crusty canine said without preamble.

"I beg your pardon?" Poe responded indignantly. It was at that very mo-ment he came to the realization that he had developed a genuine hatred for this repulsive little monster who so plagued his days.

"Look at yourself," Reynolds barked, then sniffed loudly. "*Smell* yourself. Face it, Poe—you are not fit to keep company with your fellows in the din-ing hall tonight." He made a mocking sound.

"Not that I care one bit about them or their sensitivities, you understand. But I do not wish my master to be offended by your presence."

Fighting back any one of a number of angry replies that leapt immedi-ately to his feverish but still fertile mind, Poe was forced to admit to himself that he did present a rather off-putting image.

Several days of strenuous exertions had left both him and his clothing sweat-stained and decidedly rank. Not to mention, in the case of his gar-ments, torn and dirty: though, actually, the same could just as easily have been said of his person.

"So tell me, little man," he said to his canine keeper in measured tones. "What do I do to remedy this problem?"

In reply, Reynolds opened a narrow door that Poe could have sworn was not even there a mere moment ago. It seemed to have appeared at the very moment that the second dog man—the one with the countenance of a terrier—had again vanished from sight.

Poe stepped through the doorway to find himself standing inside a small dressing room. There was fresh water, soap and large, fluffy towels atop a wash stand. On the seat of a nearby chair rested a stack of neatly folded, clean clothing.

Poe was extremely grateful for all.

While the acerbic Reynolds waited patiently or otherwise on the other side of the door, Poe stripped himself. Standing atop one of the towels, he luxuriated in a sort of sponge bath, cleansing his face, hair and body as best he could, using a fair portion of the bar of soap he had been provided. He delighted in the feel of it, though the water seemed only to slightly cool his fevered brain.

He was less thrilled with the change of clothes that had been left for his use. They were clearly made of cheap material and worn enough to be slightly frayed at the cuffs and collar. In all, they were a far, far cry from the dapper apparel that made up Poe's usual wardrobe.

Still, the garments were newly laundered and pressed, with no obvious rips or holes and for this Poe was genuinely glad. After all, one's outward appearance was quite often a reflection of what dwelt within.

Now as refreshed and clean as was possible given the limits of his resources, Poe rejoined Reynolds and was as usual shown the way to the small hall that would host the evening's repast.

He felt no surprise but still regret to see that yet another empty chair sat tilted against the dinner table. Only Candide Swan, Reverend Farr and of course Red Death himself remained to partake of supper with him.

The meal began in strained silence. The food, though seemingly well prepared, seemed rather tasteless to Poe's palate. The fact that he had difficulty swallowing it made it seem even less tempting to the tongue.

He found that when he looked at any of the candles lighting the somber affair he saw a multi-colored aura surrounding their flames. At times he thought he saw tiny figures like fairies dancing about this halo effect. He laid down his utensils and rubbed at his aching eyes.

"May I ask you a question?" he inquired of their host.

"Of course, Mr. Poe!" Red Death quickly replied, delighted that someone had at last torn the uncomfortable veil of silence that till now had hung over the table. "Anything you like."

"And will I receive an honest answer?"

Red Death chuckled. "That will depend on the question. Care to chance it?"

The author sighed. "As one of our members observed on a previous occasion, we who were drawn here are, in most respects, quite different one from the other: from different locations, of differing backgrounds.

"How is it that you even became aware of our existence?"

"How else?" Red Death replied. "The same way I know so much about those backgrounds. I was told."

"Told by whom?"

"Who else? The souls that reside within the pool."

"You commune with them?" This question was posed not by Poe but by Reverend Farr, suddenly interested in the direction the conversation had taken.

"Oh, yes."

"Often?"

"Not often, no." Red Death leaned back slightly in his chair. "After all, even one such as *I* can only bear so much sorrow and regret and anger." He made a waving motion with one hand.

"As fascinating at they can be—coming as they do from all times and all places—one can only bear their company for so long. Please don't tell them I said so."

"If communing with them is such an ordeal," Poe pressed him, "why do you do it?"

"Because…it's what I do."

"That's not much of an answer."

"It's the only one I've got."

Poe stared at him intently, nervously tapping the table top with the middle finger of his right hand.

"From what I saw," he said, "there were scores of spirits swirling around in the grip of your insidious pool."

"I wouldn't exactly call it 'mine'," Red Death replied. "It's theirs. And there are more than scores within it. There are hundreds—probably thousands.

"You see, there is no shortage of despair in this world of ours, I'm afraid, as I'm sure you would agree. Or of lost souls…both living and dead."

"Nor, I presume," Poe rejoined, "any shortage of those in some way connected to those lost souls."

"Indeed not."

"Yet of all the potential participants in this macabre game you have so skillfully engineered—you chose the eight individuals who began this contest together.

"Why us? How did you come to choose us in particular?"

"An excellent query, sir!" Red Death paused to summon his thoughts before continuing.

"In a way, you should feel flattered, I think. Not many are suited for such a challenge. It takes a very special sort of man…." He nodded toward Candide. "...Or woman." He exhaled softly.

"For example: How many people, other than yourselves, do you believe would have even entered this pleasure house of mine, hmm?

"I mean, really—think about it. An odd little man, who looks like a dog—a total stranger to you—invites you to enter a mysterious abode about which you know absolutely nothing.

"Most people would—and do—run away in the instant!"

"I see," Poe declared. "So you chose us because we were all *idiots*."

Red Death's resulting laughter was loud and hearty, accompanied by one hand lightly pounding upon the tabletop.

"Not at all, Mr. Poe—not at all." He dabbed at one eye as if his mirth had brought tears.

"I know," Candide, said, feeling the spirit to join the conversation. "It's because we are all so *brave*!"

Red Death laughed again, reaching out to pat her hand. "You *know* that isn't the case, my dear. Some of you are quite cowardly, actually."

"But there must be something," Poe continued to probe. "Some quality, some circumstance that led you to select us for this unique...opportunity."

"More than one thing, to be sure," Red Death replied. "All men and women are possessed of different qualities, the sum of which is what makes each of them unique, one from another.

"There are occasions when different qualities can lead to the same course of action. Engaging in any form of combat, physical or mental, for example, may be fueled by such diverse traits as courage, fear, love, hate, selfishness or selflessness.

"Diverse, even conflicting qualities—yet each in its way serving the same purpose.

"I think on such things greatly and I am guided by these ruminations when I select the handful who will be offered the opportunity to engage in my quaint entertainment." He cast his eyes back and forth among them.

"Each one of you—and each one of those no longer in our company—knows better than anyone what it was that prompted you to accept my offer and my terms.

"The catalysts for your decisions, of course, were the souls swirling away in my Purgatory Pool. You all felt their pull. Each of you heard, within your hearts or your minds or your souls or all three, these individual spirits crying out to you.

"What part of you most responded to their entreaties, only you know for sure. In the end, and for my purposes, your motivations matter not. Only how you respond.

"Over the years I have endeavored to recruit suitable contestants for this soulful game—and I assure you I have been at it for more years than any of you might imagine—I have become quite adept at choosing admirable competitors.

"No system, even one as meticulous as my own, is infallible, of course. From time to time, the unwilling contestant like Mr. Porter does get through the fine net I cast. But seldom so. Nor am I ever fully disappointed." Red Death paused, leaning closer to Poe.

"So don't be harsh in your judgment of either yourself or your compatriots, sir. Rather, think of yourselves as being…special."

Poe smiled sardonically. "Special. The very word we might apply to assuage the feelings of a child who is slow for his age."

Red Death again shook with mirth. "You'll not lure me into engaging in verbal swordplay with you, Mr. Poe. You're far too adept a wordsmith for me to challenge with my far humbler skills!"

Candide Swan laughed and clapped her hands. "I wasn't able to follow *any* of that!" she cheerfully admitted.

"But I'll gladly play games with any man who finds me special!" She blew a kiss to their host, then turned her attention to Sojourn Farr.

"What do *you* think, Reverend?"

The clergyman's entire head seemed to turn red with outrage. "What *I* think, you little trollop, is that it is both incomprehensible and unconscionable that good, decent men like Mr. Larou and Captain Montgomery have fallen by the wayside—while a painted tramp like *you* is still alive and well and befouling the air with her continued existence!"

"Go to Hell, Reverend!" the woman snapped, all traces of her usual coquettish charm vanished.

"I fear we may already be there, dear girl," Poe commented dryly.

"What would a dilettante like *you* know of the tortures of eternal damnation in Hell?" Farr challenged.

"Perhaps when you get there—you can send me a letter describing them," Poe replied languidly.

Candide snorted into her napkin at his words, while Farr's own response was limited to a series of indignant sputters.

"You seem to have a decidedly low opinion of religion, Mr. Poe," Red Death observed, perhaps hoping to instigate further conflict.

"Only of those who claim to practice it, sir," Poe asserted. "The pioneers and missionaries of religion have been the real cause of more trouble and war than all other classes of mankind."

"Bravo!" Candide trumpeted, raising her wineglass in a mock toast before taking a generous sip.

"Go ahead," Reverend Farr said, directing his comments at her rather than at Poe. "Make light of the Lord. You won't laugh when you feel his wrath."

"What makes you so sure I haven't *already* felt it?" Candide retorted. The slight slurring of the words indicated she was a bit in her cups.

"These last few nights alone have been Hell!"

Her comment led Poe to speculate that perhaps all the others in this game had faced similar multiple terrors of their own, such as he had experienced.

If so, each of them was probably tailored to fit the individual they had been visited upon.

And eventually, one by one, each contestant had succumbed to his or her unique horror.

As, he knew…might he.

"It's not too late for you, you know," Reverend Farr said to Candide. His hand slid across the table toward hers, but stopped short of touching it.

"You can still be saved…with the right guidance."

"I don't suppose *you'd* like to guide me, would you, Reverend?" she replied, smiling wickedly and cupping one breast in her hand invitingly.

"Good God, woman!" Farr admonished in a shocked voice. "Have you no shame at all?"

It seemed to Poe, though, that while the clergyman's voice was rife with indignation—his *eyes* lingered perhaps overly long on the woman's plunging décolletage.

"I can't afford shame," Candide said ruefully, reaching out to grasp the nearest carafe of wine and pour herself a refill.

Red Death spoke not a word, willing to be only a silent observer of what transpired. But behind his implacable mask, he smiled.

He knew the climax of this year's "entertainment" was close at hand.

CHAPTER 37

Later that night, alone in her assigned bedchamber, Candide Swan's mood had not lightened noticeably.

She sat slumped in her easy chair, with one leg thrown lewdly over its

"BRAVO!" CANDIDE TRUMPETED...

arm. In addition to a fresh glass of wine, she was indulging in yet another unladylike vice by smoking a short, thin cigar.

Her mind was in turmoil this evening. The cause of her discontent was not the seemingly supernatural dangers this bizarre setting had presented to her that weighed so heavily upon her. Her chosen…profession had led her into harrowing situations more than once.

Rather, it was the thoughts, the memories this palace of pains had evoked that so plunged her into dark melancholia.

She was of no mind to entertain any more such when she heard a gentle rapping at her chamber door.

"Go away," she snapped angrily. "Whoever—whatever—you are…just go away!"

"It's *me*, Miss Swan," a familiar, slightly wheedling voice called softly from the other side of the door.

"It's Reverend Farr!"

Candide would have doubtless been suspicious and fearful had she but known that, at the very moment he seemed to be cajoling her at her door, the Right Reverend Sojourn Farr was sitting alone in his own designated bedchamber!

As was his nightly habit (inculcated long before he came to be in this hellish place), Farr sat before his fire reading assiduously from the small Bible he carried in his coat pocket at most times.

He was poring over its pages even more fervently than usual on this night. Every evening since agreeing to participate in these bizarre "games," he had been haunted by strange dreams and visions: highly disturbing ones.

"The Lord himself was tempted by Satan," he murmured aloud, "and He, too, prevailed."

He started in fear as the distinct sound of knocking at his door intruded upon his reflections.

He remained seated, eyes firmly closed, clutching his Bible even more tightly as his tremulous lips uttered a prayer.

"The Lord is my Shepherd…."

But the praying stopped and his eyes snapped open as he heard a sultry voice call to him from without.

"Open up, Reverend. It's me…

"Candide Swan!"

Even as these twin impossibilities were seeming to take place simultaneously, Edgar Poe was ensconced in his own bedchamber. He stood before the fire, staring glumly at its dancing flames while inwardly dueling with a plethora of dark thoughts.

"Edgar," a faint voice called to him softly.

Poe spun from the fireplace the instant he heard the sound, his senses alert for whatever new danger was about to present itself.

At first, he saw nothing but darkness; his eyes, after staring into the bright flames of the fireplace, needed time to adjust to the relative gloom of the rest of the room. Time he knew would leave him vulnerable to attack.

But no attack came.

As his pupils gradually dilated he became able to see the outline of a shadowy figure standing on the opposite side of the chamber.

"What fresh demon from Hell is this?" he thought within his mind. He swallowed hard, feeling pinpricks of pain deep in his throat as he did so.

"Why are you here, Edgar?" the mysterious figure asked, even as it began to almost glide slowly toward where the writer stood transfixed.

Poe's heart began to beat more rapidly within his chest as he quickly realized the apparition presenting itself to him was decidedly *female*.

"Why are you here?" the ghost repeated, its voice quivering as if the words were being spoken into the wind.

The female figure stepped close enough to fall into the circle of light given off by the flames behind Poe, and as it did its features became starkly clear enough for him to see plainly.

"Virginia?" he gasped incredulously.

Yet this was not really a question he needed to ask or to have answered. Without doubt, he was gazing upon the thin, sad face of his wife.

His wife…who had been dead for two, long years.

CHAPTER 38

Candide Swan felt almost giddy with triumph as she flipped the remains of her cigar into the flames of her fireplace.

A large mirror had been conveniently hung upon one wall of her bedchamber, as had been the case every night during her stay here. And as had also been the case, ever since her nearly fatal encounter with mirrors on a previous night, Candide had turned it to the wall immediately upon being ushered into her room.

Knowing she now had a male caller, though, she dared slowly and cautiously to turn the mirror back around.

Seeing only her normal face looking back at her, she now took stock of herself in its glistening surface.

Self-delusion on occasion being a wonderful gift, she thought the face that looked back at her was as young and free of lines as she chose to imagine; as always, she either failed to see any blemishes or was able to excuse them away as a trick of the lighting or a normal feature of her face.

She smoothed her hair and straightened her dress, adjusting its bodice in a manner meant to reveal even more of the fullness of her ample bosom. She moistened her painted lips with her tongue and pinched both cheeks to add attractive color to them.

Foolishly throwing all caution to the wind, she flounced over to the door of the chamber and—mindless of the repeated warning Red Death had given them all—flung it open.

Upon doing so, she found it was indeed Reverend Farr she saw standing on the other side of her threshold. Or so it seemed.

"May I come in?" he asked reticently, a decidedly sheepish expression on his face.

The fallen woman smiled. She was, in all honesty, not terribly surprised to see the clergyman here, asking for entrance.

In the time she had spent at her chosen profession, she had made the acquaintance of more than one moral crusader…and had so often found them to be slaves to the same base urges and appetites as every other man as to have developed a harshly cynical opinion of the entire gender.

"By all means," she said in a slightly weary voice, stepping to one side and with a wave of her hand inviting Farr to enter.

She would not have been so foolishly complacent had she been able to see that at that very moment the actual Sojourn Farr was ensconced in his own bedchamber.

Sweat was beginning to form in small beads on the minister's broad forehead as he warily approached the locked door of his room. The tapping on the far side of it had continued unabated.

"What do you want, woman?" he demanded gruffly. He had stopped inches short of the portal, the dire warnings of Red Death echoing in his skull.

"I need help, Reverend," a weak and pleading voice replied from beyond.

"Help? Are you injured? Sick?"

"Sick in my soul," the womanly voice replied. "Like you tried to tell me. The kind of sickness that needs a godly man such as yourself to heal."

Someone who apparently knew no better had once observed that vanity's name was woman. Perhaps this self-appointed philosopher had known few men in his sheltered life, else he would surely have known they were equally susceptible to this character flaw's siren call.

Fully in its thrall, Reverend Farr smiled rather smugly, quite firmly convinced that his pious exhortations had finally found fertile soil in the soul of this wanton woman.

Besides, he told himself, it was his solemn *duty* to provide solace and guidance to any whom genuinely requested it.

Having quite equally convinced himself of his correctness, Farr swung the door of the chamber open—and found his breath catching loudly in his throat.

Candide Swan (for such it appeared to be) stood just beyond the threshold of the doorway, striking what even the most sheltered man of the cloth would recognize as being a seductive pose. The filmy nightgown, which was all that she wore, revealed more of her shapely figure than did it conceal. Farr gulped audibly and clutched his Bible more tightly to his bosom.

"Come in, child," he said in a slightly tremulous voice.

In yet a third bedchamber, Edgar Poe stood utterly transfixed by the sight of a different spectral woman. He did so, though, with much more purity of heart than did the Right Reverend.

The vision that presented itself to Poe's eyes was not that of the willowy girl of thirteen he had first married. It was a union that had appeared scandalous to some, perhaps most who knew of its full nature. In addition to being young Virginia Clemm's cousin, at age twenty-six Edgar was twice her age and a fully developed adult. Neither fact had deterred or dimmed his desire to take her to wife.

It was not the girlish image she had presented on their wedding day that now displayed itself in the gloom of his room. Yet neither was it the lovely and supple young woman into which she had blossomed in the fullness of time.

But the spectral image he saw clearly *was* that of his Virginia; of that, Poe had no doubt. It ripped at his perhaps too sensitive heart to see that this was the Virginia who had ended her tragically brief life ravaged by the miseries of consumption. Signs of her wasting were evident: the ghost woman's face was gaunt and wan, her eyes mere pricks of light sunken and nearly lost within deep, dark sockets.

Yet even though this was so, there was still an undeniable beauty about her: one that even death could not dispel or fully corrupt.

"Why are you here?" the specter once more demanded of Poe, its voice now taking on a harder and more finely honed edge.

"I'm trying to save you, Virginia," Poe moaned in anguish.

"Save me?" she retorted, her gray and lifeless lips curling up in a sneer of derision.

"Why would you want to save me?" she inquired in puzzlement.

"After all, Edgar…it was *you* who condemned me in the first place!"

CHAPTER 39

Reverend Farr backed away stiffly, mouth agape, as the simulacrum of Candide Swan advanced into his bedchamber with sensual strides.

"What are you doing, girl?" he practically croaked.

"Isn't it obvious?" she replied, smiling and shaking her head. "I'm here because I want you, Sojourn."

"Good Lord!"

"Oh, I fought it," she confessed. "I'm sure you know I did. But there's just such a feeling of *power* about you."

"The—the power of the Lord," he professed.

"The power of *you*," she corrected. "It's very appealing. You must know that."

"Be that as it may," he huffed, clinging at least tenuously to his beliefs, "we mustn't give in to our baser desires."

"Never?" she asked breathlessly.

"Only within the sacred bonds of marriage," he blustered. "And then only for purposes of procreation."

"Really? You've never strayed from that?"

The man was sweating more profusely. "We all…we all succumb to sin, my dear. All of us are flawed and imperfect. But we have to fight against our wicked natures."

"I'm tired of fighting, Sojourn. Aren't you?"

"The struggle is never ending," he replied weakly. "But we must never surrender."

Still, the man of the cloth offered no real resistance when the supposed Candide took his head in her hands and planted her full lips upon his.

It was a pleasure he had forsaken for a very long time, even with his wife, and he found himself succumbing to it with humiliating quickness.

Farr moaned low in his throat as he felt himself begin to respond physically to the touch of the woman's lush body pressing tightly against his own, to the warmth and taste of her tongue inside his mouth.

He barely noticed at first when the touch of her hands became subtly rougher and more callused.

He stiffened, though, as he suddenly felt the prick of light bristles against the skin of his face.

Farr jerked his head back sharply and was appalled beyond imagining when he saw not the soft, feminine form of Candide Swan—but that of his own young adult *son*, Jeremy. The boy smiled sarcastically at his sire.

"Abomination!" Farr screamed, harshly pushing the youth back away from him.

He stood, trembling with outrage, staring at the boy. Jeremy looked just as Farr remembered him from when he was still *alive*. He was slight of build, with soft features marred only by a nose a tad too prominent. His brown hair was thick and rolled down his neck to his slender shoulders.

The spectral lad's smile turned into an exaggerated frown.

"Abomination, Father? Isn't that just what you called me when you caught me in the hayloft with that other poor boy?"

"And rightly so," Farr replied coldly, regaining some of his composure and with it his sense of self-righteousness.

"I pleaded with you," Jeremy said, taking a step closer but then stopping when he saw his father flinch at the prospect of his nearness.

"No...I *begged* you to help me understand the desires I felt so strongly, the feelings I found to be so overwhelming.

"But you gave me no understanding, no guidance. You didn't even make an effort to help me possibly suppress those feelings."

Rather than respond to the boy's plaintive accusations, Farr simply fell to his knees. He clutched his Bible in both hands and began to mumble a prayer fervently.

"The only thing you *did* give me," Jeremy continued, unmindful of his father's mutterings, "was the back of your hand.

"Remember? It was the same night you damned me to Hell and threw me out of your house! And the next day you publicly condemned me from your bloody pulpit—assuring that every other hand would likewise be turned against me."

Farr's head snapped up as the spectral Jeremy drew closer and jerked open the collar of his simple linen shirt.

A red, swollen abrasion was clearly visible on his throat, circling it. A large, angry knot bulged from one side of his neck, just below the left ear.

"Look at it, Father!" he lashed out when Farr made to avert his eyes.

"You refused to look at it the day you found I'd hanged myself from a rafter in the very barn where you had caught me in the act.

"You ordered your servants to cut me down rather than soil your own holy hands. Ordered them to throw me into a shallow, unmarked grave. You didn't even say any words over my cold corpse."

"You took your own life," his father replied bluntly. "God's greatest gift. You could not be buried in sanctified soil."

"Shut up, you sanctimonious fraud!" Jeremy yelled. So close was he now to his father that though spectral in substance his breath seemed to wash warmly over Farr's face.

In response, the clergyman gripped his Bible more tightly and began to pray more rapidly and abjectly.

"I am your servant, God," he pled. "Save me from this horror."

"Listen to you," Jeremy sneered. "Even now, you pray for *yourself*—not for me!"

"That's because I was *right!*" Farr snapped back, his righteous indignation supplanting his fear of the ghostly manifestation of his dead son.

"Don't you *see*, boy? You were beyond the pale, beyond the power of prayer to redeem: my prayers or anyone else's.

"Your godless, shameless bestiality…your taking of your own life. You doomed *yourself* to the eternal fires of Hell!"

The smile again returned to Jeremy's lips: one devoid of any humor. "But, clearly—that's not where I *am*, is it, Father?

"You were wrong—and you know you were wrong!"

"I wasn't wrong," Farr moaned as if chanting a mantra. "I wasn't wrong. I wasn't. Don't you see? Don't you see?"

Jeremy blinked, his features contorting with sudden realization.

"My God. I *do* see, Father."

"All this that you agreed to. Whatever trials and tribulations you've endure these past few days. You haven't done this to *save* my soul –

"You want to make sure it gets sent on to Hell!"

"Where it belongs! Where the flames will consume you!" Farr screamed at the ghost of his son, flecks of his spittle flying from his lips.

"Not by my doing, but by your own. In accordance with the scriptures that govern us all. It's *God* who damns you, boy—not *I!*"

Farr's voice and eyes lowered. "The flames…they'll consume you, boy."

"No, you pompous, judgmental hypocrite," Jeremy hissed. As he leaned in even closer to his cringing father, Farr squeezed his eyes shut and turned his face away.

"They'll consume *you!*"

Though ephemeral in nature, the ghost of Jeremy Farr was still able to lay hands on his father's collar. At first, the minister offered little resistance as the spirit began to drag him roughly across the hardwood floor of the bedchamber. He simply wept as he rapidly muttered quotations from the Bible's *Book of Leviticus.*

It was only when he began to feel fully the heat emanating from the fireplace toward which he was being dragged that he came out of his stupor and began to squirm.

His struggles quickly escalated as he came to fully realize the fate his vengeful son had in store for him. His legs thrashed wildly. Dropping his Bible, he tried to claw at the specter with his hands, but found no firm flesh that might yield to his digging nails.

"You can't do this," he whined pitifully.

"I don't seem to be having much difficulty so far, Father."

"Don't, Jeremy." Tears were streaming down Farr's cheeks. "Please… show some mercy."

"I'll show you the same mercy you granted me—*Reverend*!" the ghostly avenger hissed loudly.

He then thrust his father headfirst into the hungry flames of the fireplace.

The smell of his own hair burning was the first sensory sensation Farr registered, seconds before the pain of fire lapping at the skin beneath the hair elicited an agonized scream from his lips.

He tried to push his way back out of the fire only to find that the specter that had consigned him to this horrible demise was still holding him firmly in its grips.

Immune to the fire, the ghost kept pushing Farr forward, is if feeding a log into the flames.

Farr's screams of agony did little more than suck the fire into his lungs, so that he began to roast both within and without.

His flesh was already melting like candle wax before he fully expired.

CHAPTER 40

Candide Swan faintly heard the real Sojourn Farr's screams, but she paid them no mind. To her, such disturbing sounds had become almost commonplace since first she entered this monument to the macabre.

In this moment, her mind was more absorbed in what she viewed as being but the latest in her long line of carnal conquests; reveling in the lustful looks cast her way by the personage she *thought* was Reverend Farr.

"What brings you to my room, Reverend?" she asked coyly. She was in no hurry, planning to take her time and thoroughly enjoy her successful seduction of the clergyman.

From a very early age, when a pawing man had first tried to lay hands on her when she was just a child, Candide had found she enjoyed the power her physical charms gave her over the many men with whom she had slept.

"Are you here to try to save my soul?" she whispered.

"No." Farr's reply was barely audible. His eyes fairly bulged from his head and his tongue licked his lips as if hoping to assuage a great thirst.

"No?" Candide expected she would derive a special pleasure from this particular prey.

A plan was already formulating in her mind. She would bring him slowly, almost painfully to the brink of satisfying the base and decidedly unspiritual urges that seemed to control all men—then laugh in his pious face, reject him and send him away unsatisfied and defeated.

The very thought stimulated what little remained of her own true sensual desires. Some was still contained within her heart, though; for the shadow of an instant she found herself wishing it had been Edgar Poe who had come scratching at her door rather than the Right Reverend.

"Why *are* you here, then, Reverend?" she said disingenuously to Farr, setting her sights on the target at hand.

"You know why," he replied meekly.

"I'm not sure I do. You had better tell me."

"Please," he moaned. "Don't make me do that."

Smiling, Candide ran the fingertips of her right hand up and down the valley formed by the swell of her breasts. She was pleased by the obvious effect this had on the minister.

"Is *this* why you're here?"

Farr swallowed hard. "You know it is."

"Yes," she replied with a trace of sadness mixed with weariness. "I know."

She started to slowly turn away, but crooked one finger in Farr's direction.

"Just follow me."

As Candide began to stroll toward the chamber's large, beckoning bed, her full hips swayed alluringly up and down in a practiced movement.

As she walked, experienced fingers plucked at the buttons running down the front of her dress.

"You'll be glad you came, Reverend," she said breathlessly. "I'll make sure of that. It will be a night you'll never forget."

Shrugging her shoulders out of the dress, she allowed it to fall in folds around her feet. She was clothed now in nothing save the flimsiest of undergarments, its diaphanous fabric clinging tightly to every swell and curve of her ripe body. With her back still to her nocturnal visitor, her hands moved to her shoulders, then slid languidly down her arms.

"Are you ready?"

Her lids were nearly closed, her tempting lips formed in a pout as she turned back around toward the minister.

An audible gasp gushed from her mouth; her eyes grew wide with surprise and dismay.

"*Daddy!*"

A man still faced her, just a few feet away—but he looked nothing at all like the plump and prosperous Reverend Sojourn Farr.

This man looked to be years older than Farr, though this was likely an illusion brought on by the features of a man grown worn and old before his time by the wasting effects of hard work.

Both his skin and the tattered clothing that barely clung to his skeletal body were filthy—caked in the dust of the Pennsylvania coal mines in whose stygian bowels he had labored for bone crushing decades—and inside which he had *died*.

"Hello, Myrtle," the ghost of Horace Swan said, in a voice that had long since left mere fatigue behind. Even now, as he spoke, fine particles of the choking coal dust rose from his lungs and were expelled from his lifeless lips.

Candide gasped again, the sound almost a sob. This was the first time anyone had spoken her real name since she had left home longer ago that she cared or dared to recall.

"You look terrible, Daddy."

There was a note of genuine concern in her voice; yet so deeply ran her current state of moral dissipation that it did not occur to her to try to cover her near nakedness in the presence of her father.

"I looked a lot worse by the time the *Black Lung* took me," he replied somberly. Even here, inside his daughter's bedchamber, his voice echoed slightly, as if the words were being spoken within some cavernous depth.

"But you wouldn't know that, would you, Myrtle? You were long gone by then." He sighed, and dark dust drifted from his nostrils.

"You didn't even bother to return for my funeral."

Despite the words, there was no tone of accusation in the specter's voice. Only sadness.

"I—I didn't know," Candide murmured, sounding transparently unconvincing even to her own ears.

"Oh, you knew, child," the ghost of Swan replied. "Your mother sent you word."

Before responding to having the lie thrown back in her face, Candide nervously fished a silver case from a pocket of her discarded dress, reaching for another thin cigar. She coughed twice lightly when she took her first puff of it.

"I wondered about that," she said, appearing to be unfazed that this image of her father had seen through her attempt at deception.

"How did she know where I was?"

"Oh, poor Myrtle," the ghost replied dolefully. "*Everybody* knew. Word of you and your…activities was widespread. Your mother knew all too well where you were."

"And how is Mommy?" Candide asked: not from any genuine concern or even simple curiosity, but only as an attempt to divert the course of the conversation.

"Do you care, girl?"

Candide stared at him, nervously tapping one foot while clicking together the nails on the thumb and forefinger of her left hand.

"No," she finally said, her voice as cold as indifference. It was one of the few truths she had told in a long, long time.

"Why should I?" she snapped, anger and defensiveness winning out over her initial fear in the presence of the specter.

She again coughed, this time from the fine particles of coal dust her father continued to expel with every breath of his phantom lungs. Candide dispelled them with an impatient wave of her hand.

"By the time I left home," she said harshly, "I couldn't stand the sight of her." She took a deep drag from her cigar.

"Her and every other woman I saw day after day after day. You wonder why I ran away, Daddy? *That's* why." She shook her head contemptuously.

"So I wouldn't become just like them…poor, hopeless, old before their time. Worn down to nothing. Less than nothing."

"And you felt your only other option was to debase yourself?" her father asked. Again, the expression on his face was one of sorrow rather than of judgment.

"Why shouldn't I do what I do?" Candide shot back. From the time I was just a little girl, I saw the way men looked at me. I knew what they *really* wanted—and it wasn't *love*." She drew herself up taller, a haughty look on her face.

"So, why shouldn't I make them *pay* for the pleasure?"

The look on the specter's pale face in reaction to this, she found, hurt more than could any mere words. Her father lifted his eyes to survey the boundaries of the bedchamber.

"And what about here and now, Myrtle?" he asked her. "What sort of *payment* are you hoping to receive from what you are doing here and now? Why are you doing this?"

Candide blinked. "Why…I'm trying to free your poor soul from that dreadful pool, Daddy. Why else?"

The ghost of Swan again shook its head sadly. "Try to be honest again, Myrtle, at least to yourself. Since when have you cared about the state of anybody's soul—including your own?"

She stared back at him in rage, then twisted at the waist to throw the remnant of her cigar into the flames of the fireplace before forming any verbal response to his words.

"Fine!" she nearly screamed, once more waving away at the cloud of coal dust that grew heavier as the ghost of her father stepped closer to his wayward daughter.

"Have the *truth*, then, old man—if you prefer it." Rage had overwhelmed any sense of dread Candide might have felt in the presence of this manifestation of the otherworldly.

"You think I don't *know* how other people see me? How they look down their noses at me for who I am and what I do? Even people like you and Mommy—and all the other filthy, ignorant moles content to live in the slagheaps.

"And what do you have to show for all of your 'honest' labors? A mountain of debt owed to the company store. Packs of hungry children you bring into a world that will be as gray and hopeless for them as your own: children whose only inheritance will be the same kind of slow death that finally claimed you." She was shaking with anger.

"But I don't even get my feet dirty, because I can afford to hire a carriage. I have money and all the things that money can buy. I have a good life, a comfortable life."

"What about other people's lives, Myrtle?" the spectral image of her father asked.

"What do you mean?"

"I wasn't the only one you left behind, remember? What about your mother? Your brothers and sisters? Did it ever once occur to you to use your wealth to help them—to help make their lives more bearable?"

Candide's sculpted brows furrowed deeply. "No, Daddy; it never did. Mommy made her choice as to the kind of life she wanted to live—just as I made mine." Her look changed to one of triumph.

"And how much *more* satisfying will that life be," she concluded, punctuating her words with a sneer, "if you come to owe the salvation of your very soul to the actions of a *whore*!"

Her ghostly sire's head snapped back as if Candide had physically struck him. The forlorn expression on his face was even more pronounced.

"Is that it?" he said dolefully. "In the end...do you hate me *that* much, child?"

In the face of his sorrow, Candide's own features softened for just a heartbeat or two. Then they grew cold and insolent once more.

"I hate what you *are*, Daddy," she said through clenched teeth. "Or what you *were*. You and dear old Mommy both."

"And what was that?" the specter replied. "What were we? Two people who loved each other and did our best to make a good life together?"

"You consider what you had to be a good life?" Candide shot back, frankly astounded. "Back-breaking, soul-crushing years spent groveling in the dirt and working yourselves into an early grave?" She shook her head fiercely.

"Well, I want none of that!" She made a haughty, scoffing sound.

"So, here's what's going to happen, Daddy. I'll do whatever it takes to drag you out of that damned pool you got yourself trapped in—and then I'm through with you for once and for all!"

The ghost's eyes narrowed in a fashion that should have served as a warning. "Aren't you forgetting something very important, Myrtle?"

"What might that be?"

"The only way you can achieve that goal—is by *winning* that ungodly contest you've entered into."

Candide laughed mockingly at this, only to have the laugh end in another, stronger and more ragged cough. This time, it felt as if something had been expelled from within her.

She wiped the back of her right hand across her mouth—and found it came away smeared with a black smudge.

A series of deep, rapid coughs racked her shapely body. It felt as though something had been lodged deep down in her throat, making it difficult to draw oxygen into her lungs.

"What's happening to me?" she gasped.

"You're beginning to experience my pain, child," the spectral Horace Swan replied tonelessly. Candide was starting to feel like she was somehow drowning in her own fluids.

"Help me, Daddy!" she wheezed, but the ghostly image of her father stood unmoved and unmoving, staring sadly at his struggling daughter.

Candide dropped to her knees, both hands clutching at her throat as it became increasingly difficult to suck life-sustaining air into her heaving bosom.

A sickening, gurgling sound rose from within her, as her body began to jerk and convulse uncontrollably.

She threw her head back and from her gaping, gasping mouth oily, wet sludge bubbled up and out like the waters of a small geyser.

The slimy goo shot upward only to fall back down onto her face, sliding over and covering her once lovely features.

This mystic mixture continued to erupt out and fall back down in copious streams. The flow did not stop until her entire writhing and wriggling body was covered in sludge—which then began to harden almost instantly.

When the process ended, Candide Swan was frozen in the shape of a pleading supplicant—looking like a statue carved by gifted but twisted hands into a bizarre statue chiseled from a single, enormous block of shiny black coal.

The image of her father looked upon his handiwork not with triumph but with sadness. Then the ghost dispelled like a wisp of smoke in the wind, returning to the soul in the pool that was the true source of its existence.

CHAPTER 41

Edgar Poe was dumbfounded by the accusation that had been spat at him by the spirit of his dead wife.

"I don't understand," he managed to stammer. "How can you say that I condemned you?"

"It's simple truth, Edgar," the ghost explained. "You see, in order for a soul to be at *rest*—it must first be at *peace*."

"I still don't understand," he replied, though in fact he felt sickeningly sure that he was beginning to.

"Did you really think I was unaware of the other women, Edgar?" Vir-

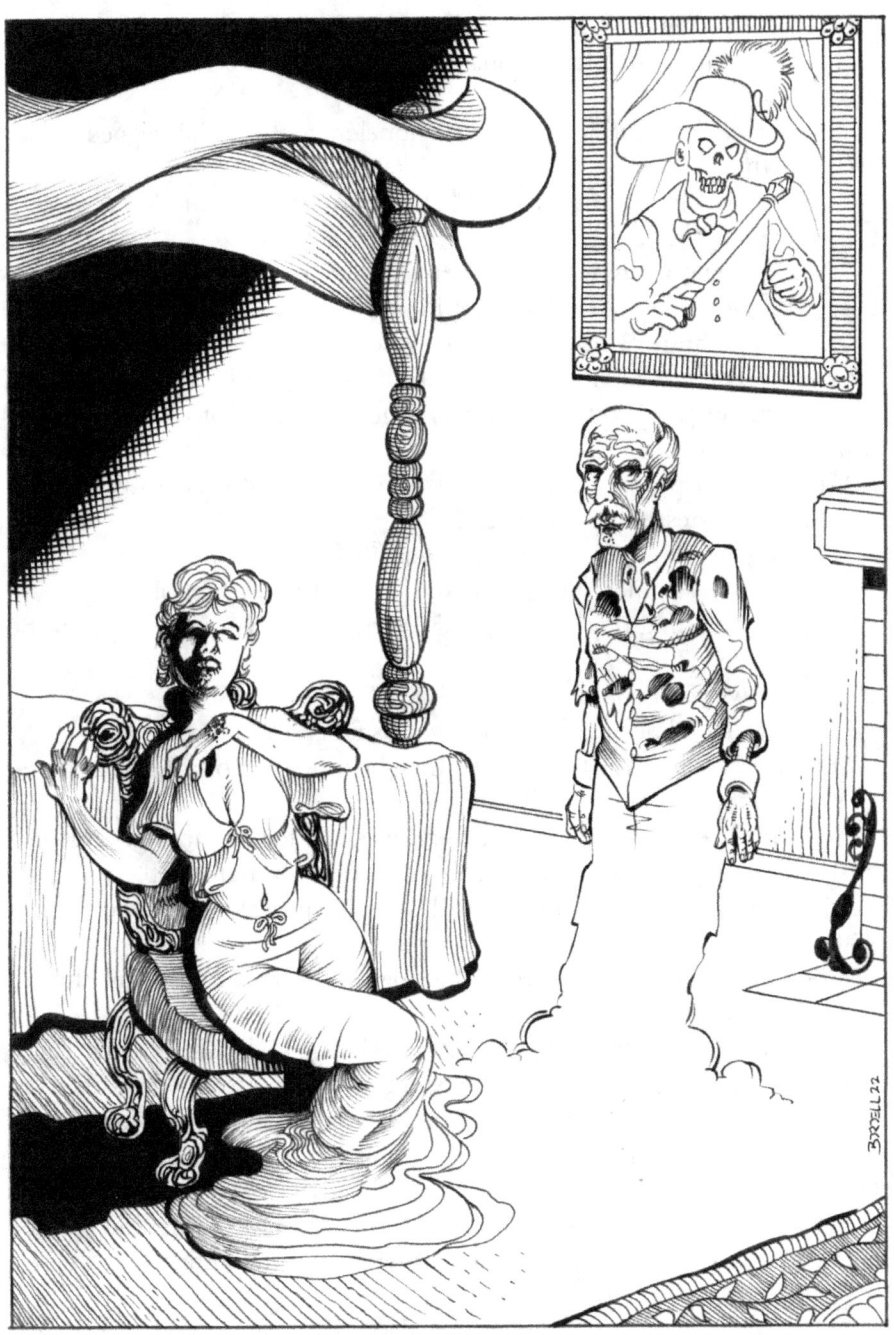

"What's happening to me?"

ginia said, shaking her head slowly back and forth. "Is that another lie you convinced yourself was true to justify not waiting until I was at least cold in the ground?"

Poe waved his hand in the air in a hopeless gesture that begged her to go no further.

"At least be honest now, dearest," she continued. "While I was *dying*—you were *dallying.*"

"Please," he now uttered aloud, burning with shame along with his growing fever. "Don't say it like that, Virginia!"

"How else should I say it?" she retorted. "Is it *your* feelings that need most to be assuaged?" The spirit's tiny, translucent hands doubled into fists.

"My God, Edgar…you brought that Osgood woman into our very home while I was still alive!

"For what purpose, pray tell? Did you truly think it was fitting for your *wife* to play hostess to your *mistress*?

"Or did you simply do it to further humiliate me?"

"No, no, no, Virginia," Poe groaned. "I swear that wasn't so!"

"On our wedding day," she replied in icy tones, "you also swore to be faithful to me.

"Your vows don't count for much, Edgar."

The writer said nothing; for once, words failed the wordsmith.

"But at least you didn't leave me," the ghost pressed on. "You remained with me to the end.

"You don't really know what that end was like for me, though, my dear husband. The growing weakness, the helplessness. Barely able to move; wetting myself like a newborn baby. The humiliation at having you witness that."

Poe's clenched fists pounded at the sides of his head as if in an effort to unhear her words.

"Mostly, there was the *fear*," she continued unabated. "The fear that came again and again, every time my lungs began to fill with my own diseased essence. It was like drowning over and over again. Like being held under water against your will until at last your struggles ended and life fled." Her features twisted even more in fury.

"And my last conscious thought before I left the flesh behind me forever…was that *yours* were the hands holding me under, Edgar!"

"Oh, God," Poe moaned.

"Yet I suppose I wasn't totally blameless," the specter said to him, unmindful of his obvious misery.

"From very early on, even before you achieved fame, I was aware of the many temptations that were thrown in your path. I convinced myself that I should feel honored that my husband was such a desirable man…and so I said nothing, did nothing. I looked the other way until at last there was no other way.

"And after all, you did not have to succumb to those temptations so easily—or so often.

"Even now," she accused, "while one woman patiently waits in ignorant bliss for your return—you were on your way to another!"

"No," Poe said weakly. "It wasn't like that."

"Then, what was it like, Edgar? Tell me, won't you? Make me understand. I would really like to know. Tell me, was it my fault? Was I lacking as a wife, a lover in some important way? Did I drive you into infidelity?"

Poe opened his mouth to reply, but wisely stopped himself before uttering any words he surely would have regretted in the instant that he spoke them. His shoulders slumped and he lowered his head, unable to meet the specter's judgmental gaze.

"No," he finally, feebly admitted. "No guilt can accrue to you, Virginia. Nor can I lay any claim to innocence.

"Every accusation you could hurl at me, and more—is true. I was weak and gave in to that weakness.

"I deserve whatever form of condemnation you choose to visit upon my head…and more."

Having thus made his painful confession, he again lifted up his face to her, his heart rending at the doleful expression on her fragile face.

"But it was always you and only you that I truly loved," he insisted. "I loved you from the moment I first laid eyes on you, when you were little more than a child."

His profession brought only a sneer to the specter's lips. "And since when is love expressed by betraying the object of that love?" she demanded of him.

"And when did this love you swear to have felt for me begin to wither away and die?"

"Never!" he declared adamantly. "A love such as I felt for you can never be gotten over!"

"Oh. It can only be spread around, is that it, Edgar?"

"No," Poe said meekly, any defenses he had crumbling to dust. "It can only be cherished—or betrayed." His body trembled as he sharply drew in a deep breath.

"And I betrayed yours."

The specter stared at him in silence for a full minute before responding. "And tell me, Edgar…do you expect me to absolve you of your sins?"

"No, darling. I don't. I don't deserve absolution. Or understanding…or forgiveness."

"What is it you want, then? I ask again: why are you here?"

"I'm trying at last to make amends, Virginia—in the only way it seems I can.

"By struggling with all my might to win this otherworldly contest and by so doing give you the peace in death that I deprived you of in life. That's why I've kept going, despite all the obstacles I've had to overcome."

Even as he spoke of adversity, Poe felt his mind growing increasingly feverish and disoriented. Other ghostly images seemed to dance in the air around Virginia, but whether they were actually there or merely the products of delusion he could not have said with certainty.

"You know, Edgar," the specter of his wife said almost tauntingly, "there *is* a way for me to be set free from the pool even if you lose this dreadful game."

"What?" Poe found he was having some difficulty in processing his thoughts and feared he might not have heard her correctly.

"Oh, yes," Virginia told him. "That Red Death rascal—he is a canny fellow. He was clever enough not to have totally lied to you and the others he lured into his den. But he *has* deceived you." She chuckled in a sarcastic fashion.

"His was a sin of omission, I suppose you could say."

"How so?" Poe's faculties were still clear enough to realize that it might be the specter that was trying to deceive him.

"It's simple, really, and rather obvious. Red Death led you all to believe that the only way you could free a captive soul was by successfully winning your way to the end of the contest.

"But there is *another* way in which tortured souls such as mine can be released from within that swirling prison of our own design." She gave the writer a conspiratorial wink, and the meaning behind it rapidly coalesced inside his seething mind.

"Of course," he gasped hoarsely in realization. "By finding *another* soul to take your place!"

"That's right," Virginia replied. "You are a clever man, Edgar. That's just one of the many qualities I found to be attractive about you. At least until… well, you know."

"But it can't be just *any* soul, can it, Virginia?" Poe asked, the full deviltry of what she was saying finally dawning on him.

"Oh, my—no! Only a soul that is in some wise connected to your own is capable of releasing you and assuming your torment onto itself.

"Now you know exactly what happened to all the others who entered into this contest along with you, Edgar.

"That's why, day by day, there were fewer and fewer left to partake of the sumptuous dinners Red Death so enjoys hosting.

"If you were to go back and take a look into the depths of that dreadful pool, Edgar—you would see that their forfeited souls are now languishing inside it: the cowardly soldier, the cruel slave master, the grasping thief. All of them.

"Just as yours would have been had you succumbed to any of the challenges you faced before tonight.

"And the vengeful spirits that lured them to their fate are now free and moved on to their just rewards, after lingering just long enough to enjoy the sight of those who had taken their place within the miasma.

"They are free at last from the hate, anger, pain and confusion that kept them bound to this plane of existence where I still reside…for now."

"So, whether I win this competition or lose my life at your hands—your soul will be released from captivity," Poe murmured, fully realizing what the ghost had been telling him.

"Exactly."

Virginia's spectral hands suddenly shot forward, grabbing Poe by either side of his head in an icy grip that set his whole body to trembling.

They held him immobile, forcing him to gaze into the eyes of the spirit woman. In his fever-addled vision, her eyes seemed to be literally afire with burning hatred—all of it directed at him.

"Do you have any idea what it's like to be trapped day after day inside that swirling, malevolent maelstrom?" So strong was her hold on his head that he could manage neither to nod nor shake it. The ghost needed no response from him to continue.

"There, you are not only drowning in your own despair, but that of all the others. Hopelessness and hate are the main sensations, the only emotions you can really feel or recognize. Whatever caused your physical death, its pain is revisited upon you twofold. With no surcease, no relief."

If the specter had plunged a dagger into Poe's heart and twisted it, it would have caused him no more agony than did her words.

"Oh, Edgar. Wallowing in the pool may not be as horrible as being continually consumed in the furnace of Hell...but it is torture nonetheless." An aching groan escaped from the ghost's lips.

"Sorrow, Edgar...that's what it is. Sorrow such as no living soul could bear without plunging at last into madness and death." Virginia's spectral hands fell away from Poe's face, dropping limply to her sides.

"Only...we in the pool are not allowed to die. Because we're already dead, you see?" Poe could feel her pain flowing out from her ghostly form in steady waves.

"And it's not just your own pain that you feel over and over. So crowded together are we in that pool to which we have been consigned that each soul there also feels the sorrows and losses of all the other souls in addition to its own.

"The turmoil felt by Christ Jesus, alone in the Garden of Gethsemane— that is how I would describe the sorrows of those inside the pool." Her next words came out almost as a sob, a soft wail of one lost in the wilderness.

"And it is a sorrow that never ends!"

Ephemeral arms wrapped around an equally tenuous body as if to hold it together. "Can you understand now," she continued, "why it might be so much more satisfying if I was to trade places with you rather than allow you to release me by virtue of having won Red Death's churlish game?"

"I do," Poe said softly.

"Do you really, Edgar?" she almost snarled. "If you survive, if you reach your goal, win this game, it will free me, surely.

"But it would also leave you free as well. Free to go on enjoying all that life has to offer...an opportunity that was denied to me." Her voice grew more strident, more insistent.

"And believe me—*every* soul in that pool feels the same way I do," she asserted.

"That's why, while the goal of you and the others has been to reach the end of this obstacle course—*our* goal has been to destroy our individual... 'soul mates.'

"Because by doing that, rather than cheering you on to victory or even taking an active hand in ensuring such—we could condemn you to take our places within the pool while our souls would finally be free. Free and content that we had achieved our revenge against those who had so wronged us in life.

"That's why, using what little autonomy and power we possessed, we instead aided and abetted those challenges Red Death had set to bar your paths. We sent out manifestations of our hatred, our torment—such as the one that you now gaze upon—to haunt each of you. To haunt and, if we were successful, to plunge you forever into the same nightmare inside which we had been contained!"

If the ghostly woman had expected a violent reaction to this declaration, she was doomed to disappointment. Poe had again lowered his eyes and bowed his head, but he did not so much as flinch from the sting of her words. She glared at him in silent puzzlement until he at last raised his face back up to hers.

"Do it, Virginia," he murmured in defeat.

"What?"

Poe merely stared at the specter dully, though his usually expressive eyes did begin to fill up with tears.

They blurred his vision slightly, for which he was actually grateful—for this effect made Virginia's gaunt and tormented features seem to soften so as to more closely resemble the vibrant, beautiful face upon which he had so often happily gazed until the consumption had robbed her of both.

"Kill me," he said flatly, no inflection at all in his voice.

The ghost hissed sharply, as if his words were acid that had been flung into its incorporeal face.

"You don't mean that, Edgar."

"Oh, but I most surely do, darling," he replied, his voice strengthening as he became ever more sure of his decision.

"After all," he said, "you are absolutely in the right. I am totally to blame for the fact that you were unable to find in death the peace and comfort that was missing from your life at the end.

"You didn't then—and you don't now—deserve to be denied such a simple reward, through no fault of your own.

"I know you won't believe me when I say this—and there is no reason that you should—but I do truly love you. I always have and I always will.

"But that declaration of devotion—whether it be true or only a base lie—does not alter the fact that I stand guilty as accused. I betrayed that love. I betrayed you. Because I was weak." Poe drew in a deep breath, then slowly exhaled it as he straightened to his full height.

"I feel a sort of contentment, now," he told the ghostly vision, "and I'm fully prepared to prove my love for you—by sacrificing my own immortal soul."

"Just like that?" the spirit rejoined. "No hesitation? No fear?"

"Oh, I'm quite full of fear, Virginia. I always have been." He actually managed to give her a wisp of a smile.

"And this time, it's well founded, I imagine." He shook his head slightly. "For I think that, unlike you, once I consign my spirit to that dreadful pool—it will remain there for all eternity."

"You sound rather sure of that, Edgar."

"I am, Virginia. As I said, I suspect that unlike you I have no one among the living who cares enough for me to make such a sacrifice as this to set my darkened soul free.

"Also unlike you, I will have been condemned by my own actions—and have no one else to blame for my awful fate. No one I could rightly wish to risk oblivion on my behalf."

The specter's face showed its puzzlement when the object of its wrath then literally chuckled softly.

"Nor is there anyone I despise so much that I would take pleasure in luring them to their doom to save myself," Poe told her.

"Not even Longfellow." He chuckled again. "Or that horrid Rufus Griswold, for all his loathsome attempts at verse."

Poe could not know that it was his literary rival Reverend Rufus Griswold who would be largely responsible in the years to come for pushing the characterization of Poe as a totally dissolute personage.

Nor, in this most critical moment, would it have mattered if Poe had known. He was too tired, too sick, and too certain of his ultimate fate to give even passing thought to such matters.

"That's it, then?" the spectral Virginia said, suspicion plainly evident in her voice.

"No pleading for mercy? No effort to justify your past deeds now that you've been called to account?" She leaned in closer to him, taking pleasure in seeing him flinch at her ghostly nearness.

"No pitiful attempt to strike a bargain with God or Satan to save yourself?"

"No," Poe replied in soft resignation.

"I deserve no mercy…so I will ask for none."

The specter gazed deeply into the writer's eyes and saw reflected there nothing but deep sorrow.

"Whether you believe me or not, darling, I do love you," he told her for the last time. "Too much to plead for a forgiveness I have not earned." He again drew himself up as straight and tall as he could manage.

"Do it," he repeated, more forcefully than before.

"Destroy me, Virginia—and free yourself!"

For all his resolve, though, he could not hide his reaction of shock as, in response to his words, the ghostly Virginia's face began to contort horribly, taking on an inhuman appearance.

Yet, as the specter's mouth opened to grotesquely impossible proportions, animalistic growls issuing forth from it, Poe tried to steel himself for whatever awful punishment was forthcoming and to which he had willingly condemned himself.

No matter what—he was determined not to relent, not to beg for surcease.

He did cry out, though, as with a sudden, ear-splitting roar, a horrendous blast of foul-smelling wind issued out of the specter's distended mouth. It struck him full in the face like a veritable tidal wave of raw sewage.

The nearly overpowering smell of decay, raw meat and excrement flooded Poe's olfactory senses, causing him to gag and his stomach to twist into tightly squeezed knots.

Rather than subside, the foul wind blasting against his face grew stronger and stronger, until it threatened to blast the very eyeballs from his head.

And then, at last, against his will—he opened his own mouth and began to scream at the top of his aching lungs.

Until darkness descended full upon him like a heavy velvet curtain, cutting off all sight, all sound and plunging him into hopeless darkness.

CHAPTER 42

The irascible little dog man Reynolds, tongue lapping at his foamy lips as always, marched smartly down the hallway leading to Edgar Poe's bedchamber the following morning.

Stopping there, he took a moment to straighten the folds of the ludicrous little suit in which he was garbed before beginning his usual, ritualistic pattern of knocking on the chamber's door.

One knock. A five-second pause. Two knocks. Another five-second pause. The same as always.

But then, in the midst of what should have been the series of three knocks, the door leading into the chamber was suddenly flung open from inside.

Caught completely off-guard and off-balance, Reynolds' next swing of his stubby fist connected with nothing but empty air and he was thrown forward, stumbling and falling to the floor flat on his face.

Stunned by this unexpected turn of events, Reynolds rolled onto his back—to see a bedraggled and wide-eyed Edgar Poe standing menacingly over him.

Reynolds' beady, ebony eyes widened as far as nature allowed them when he immediately realized that not only had his human charge somehow survived yet another night—but was now *armed* as well.

Having broken apart a ladder-backed chair that was part of the bedchamber's furnishings, Poe was now wielding one of its legs like a long truncheon.

The author now began to make deadly use of it. Before Reynolds could make the slightest defensive move, Poe brought the makeshift club down in an arching blow that flattened the dog man's nose even further. Cartilage cracked and blood sprayed from flared nostrils.

Accompanied by animalistic noises of his own, Poe almost maniacally flailed away at the supine little mongrel, screaming and yelling invectives at the canine tormentor who had become the bane of his existence.

Reynolds frantically rolled back and forth on the floor, yelping as he tried in vain to protect both head and body from the heavy blows raining down upon him. The crack of snapping bones sounded like sharp, rapid gunfire.

After what felt like an eternity to the little dog man, the deranged and violent assault ceased. Poe loomed over him, his chest heaving from his exertions, air wheezing in and out of his aching lungs.

The man stared at the bludgeon in his hand, seemingly fascinated by the sight of canine blood dripping off its stained end. His fingers then loosened their grip and the club fell to the floor. Poe slowly followed it down, to kneel beside the mortally wounded Reynolds.

The dog man, battered, broken and bleeding heavily from multiple, jagged tears in his furry skin, let out a soft, pitiful whimper.

"Still alive?" Poe said in a cold and heartless voice, bending down even closer and gazing at Reynolds with eyes gone mad.

"Too bad."

Rising unsteadily to his feet, Poe kept staring down at his fallen victim mercilessly. Unconsciously, he scratched at the still sensitive patch of skin around the spot where the vicious Reynolds had bitten him on that first day that now seemed so very long ago.

After that moment, though, he gave the dying dog man no further thought.

The little presence of mind he still retained led Poe to the room's wash basin, where he cleaned away as best he could the spatters of blood on his hands, face and secondhand clothing. He then staggered alone out of the bedchamber and into the hallway beyond. His throat felt raw and inflamed, his head was beginning to pound incessantly.

He did his best to ignore both. Having somehow survived the horrendous happenings of the previous night—how, he was not sure, for it was all a jumbled series of disconnected visions flitting through his fevered brain—Poe was determined to continue on the course he had agreed upon. His step seemed actually to be lighter without having his hated canine companion along with him, though that feeling too might have been at least partly illusory.

Today, though, as he sluggishly willed one foot after the other to step forward, he thought he saw something ahead of him that had not been visible on any other day's trek.

It appeared to be a *door* set in the wall toward which the corridor at last seemed to be leading him.

As had always been the case on this odyssey of fear, however, such things as distance were deceiving and the door proved to be not nearly so close at hand as it had at first appeared.

More than once during this long and arduous day, Poe's strength would fail him, sending him stumbling and falling to the cold, hard floor.

Each time he fell, more time was required for him to regain enough breath and will to continue. But each time he eventually pushed himself back up to his feet and staggered forward.

It was his mind as much as his body that kept him going, and he found that mind was being deteriorated by the burning fever that seemed to penetrate into and through his very skull.

This day, even more than all the taxing ones that had preceded it, seemed interminable. Such was Poe's state of utter exhaustion that he initially took no note of it when the corridor abruptly ended and he stepped beyond it into a bare but spacious foyer.

And on the side of the foyer opposite to where the author stood swaying on unsteady feet—a large and ornately carved door could indeed be seen, set firmly in the wall!

Even in his current condition, with thoughts as hard to call on as were his physical muscles, Poe realized what this hard fought for moment signified.

He had *won*.

He had faced every test, every challenge, every horror this house of pain had thrown in his path…and he had overcome them all.

Poe took one step, then another toward the beckoning door before his legs failed him yet again. He fell heavily to his hands and knees, moaning in pain.

He remained in that position for long moments, head hanging down loosely between his shoulders as he tried to suck much needed wind back into his burning lungs.

And when he at last lifted his heavy head back up—he saw the garishly garbed figure of Red Death now standing between him and his final goal.

CHAPTER 43

Neither man spoke; they merely stared in stony silence at each other. Then Red Death started to walk forward.

As he did, he raised his gloved hands…and slowly began to clap them together.

"My congratulations, Mr. Poe," the masked man said in his unique tone of voice.

"You have successfully completed the course—the only one of this year's contestants to do so." Poe still had enough presence of mind to realize that two more of his fellows must have of necessity fallen by the wayside since last night. Candide Swan and Reverend Farr must have met the same unknown fates as had all the others save he.

"You've won, sir," Red Death said in conclusion.

"But…*how*?" Poe croaked. With a supreme effort of will, he rose unsteadily and took a few steps on leaden feet to meet his approaching host.

His confusion was understandable. After all, as he now confessed to Red Death, the spirit of his lost love Virginia had not only held him totally in her power, but he had willingly surrendered to whatever form of torture and death she might rightfully have chosen to inflict upon him.

Yet when the savage and seemingly fatal whirlwind she had unleashed upon him had finally subsided, the specter had simply vanished with the sound of a sigh—leaving Poe stunned and even further disoriented.

But still alive.

Even as he finished this narrative, it occurred to Poe that his host probably already knew all this. That it was likely that in some improbable manner he had been an unseen spectator all along—viewing from a safe place of hiding not only all of Poe's travails along the way but those of the other competitors as well.

At an earlier time, this idea of such perverse voyeurism might have outraged Poe. But in his current state, the writer had no energy for such a strong emotion.

"Why?" was all he could manage to murmur. "Why, after all…did Virginia choose to spare me?"

"Perhaps," Red Death told him in reply, "in the end she forgave you for all you had done to her—and spared you from the horrible fate she had initially planned for you—because she realized you were exhibiting the one trait that made you deserving of achieving victory in my humble amusement.

"Perhaps she saw for herself that at last you had learned the crucial lesson the other competitors never did."

"What lesson might that be?" Poe stammered, uncomprehending.

As sharp as was his mental acuity under normal circumstances, the author was in this moment genuinely stymied. In his present condition of physical debilitation and fever, he was finding it increasingly difficult to concentrate.

"The lesson was simply this," Red Death told him softly.

"Merely feeling *guilt* for one's actions…is not the same as feeling *remorse*."

Red Death's voice then took on an almost paternal tone.

"Nor is it the same as taking *responsibility* for those actions."

In response, Poe found he could do nothing but stare at the masked mystery man in silence. His eyes blinked rapidly, as if in an effort to clear his vision.

"That's it, then?" he finally managed to say in a hushed voice. "Virginia's soul is free?"

"Free as a bird," Red Death replied.

"And what of me?"

"Likewise free," Red Death replied. He stepped to one side and gestured toward the nearby door.

"Allow me to say that you played the game most admirably, most splendidly, Mr. Poe. And I greatly enjoyed our conversations. I'm sad, in a way; with the course run, there will be no more opportunity for us to break bread and share philosophies. You are now free to leave my humble abode."

Poe started to head past Red Death, then paused to look over at him.

"I still don't really know who or what you are, sir," he said. "Or even what you look like."

"Ah. Curiosity—the artist's greatest muse of all, perhaps. Would you like to see the answer for yourself?" Red Death spoke casually, leaning close to the writer.

"All you have to do in order to have all your questions answered, your curiosity satisfied—is pull my mask away and see what lies revealed.

"By all means, feel free to do so if you wish."

His mind a jumble, Poe slowly raised a slightly trembling hand, meaning to do just that.

But he stayed that hand when he looked more closely into the eyes he found peering back at him through the slits in the molded crimson mask.

They were so dark that initially he saw nothing save a deep, inescapable emptiness. Then, most disturbing of all, he saw something else deep within that void.

A reflection of himself.

"No," he mumbled with a thick tongue, lowering his hand and averting his eyes.

"I think it's best I never know."

"I think you're right," Red Death replied wickedly, then again made a sweeping gesture toward the silently beckoning door.

"Now, go," he commanded in a voice that carried no harshness.

"And know that you have my sacred word on it that the very instant you step over that threshold—the soul of your loved one will be let loose and sent to her just reward."

Despite this assurance, Poe hesitated once more as his hand closed on the doorknob. One last time, he looked back at Red Death.

"Thank you," he murmured softly.

Red Death was taken slightly aback by this sentiment. "Of all the many men and women who have participated in these games of mine," he told the author, "none but you has ever said that to me."

Without another word, but with just the shadow of a smile on his lips, Poe opened the door and stepped—or, rather, staggered—out into the beckoning night beyond.

Behind him, Red Death came to stand in the open doorway, thinking thoughts suited only for him…watching Poe as he slowly made his way into the enveloping darkness.

A soft sound from behind him, a hint of movement caught in the corner of one eye caused the masked man to turn around, closing the door as he did.

He saw two of his subservient little dog men walking along the corridor. Between them they carried a diminutive stretcher, upon which lay an equally tiny figure covered by a black sheet.

At a wordless gesture from their master, they came to a halt. Stepping close to them, Red Death pulled one end of the sheet back—to find himself looking down at the lifeless body of Reynolds.

The beady eyes in the corpse's bulldog-like head were open, but there was no longer any trace of light in them. Foamy saliva had dried into a yellow crust upon lips curled back into the rictus of death from his pointed canine teeth.

"Ah, Reynolds," Red Death said, speaking to the slain canine laid out before him.

"You poor, dumb...*rabid* little brute."

He gently pulled the sheet back over Reynold's head and returned his gaze to the doorway through which Edgar Poe had made his exit mere minutes earlier.

"I *do* so hope the dismal disease carrier didn't spread his affliction by *biting* someone."

As the stretcher-bearers continued on with their lifeless burden, Red Death threw his head back and began to laugh, maniacally and loudly.

So loudly, in fact, that even some distance away the fevered Poe heard the peals of laughter as he continued to stumble through the darkness. Or at least he thought he did. He wasn't sure—for reality was beginning to take its leave from him.

He had no concept of the time or date—no idea that he was on his way to meet his final fate.

CHAPTER 44

"Lord help my poor soul."

Those were the last words to escape the lips of the living Edgar Allan Poe.

That final outburst occurred in the early morning hours of October 7, 1849. The night before, Poe—who had never become fully cognizant or coherent enough to tell anyone what had brought him to this sorry state—had again begun to mumble the name "Reynolds" over and over again in his delirium.

No witness who was on hand to hear this had the slightest idea as to what the significance of this name was.

The author's attending physician, Dr. John J. Moran, and two nurses stood and watched helplessly as, with a long and mournful exhaling of air, Edgar Poe breathed his last breath.

Poe had been lying abed inside Washington College Hospital for four days, brought there by the Good Samaritan Joseph Walker after he had encountered Poe aimlessly wandering the back alleys of Baltimore.

And now…he had uttered his final five words while upon the mortal plane.

"It's over," Dr. Moran said somberly. "He's gone."

"The poor, poor man," the younger of the two nurses commiserated. "Were you ever able to determine exactly what it was that was killing him, doctor?"

Dr. Moran shook his head slowly.

"Not with any real certainty. For now, my journal will simply list cause of death as congestion of the brain."

He turned his attention to the older of the nurses. "Were we able to find and notify any next of kin, Miss Atkins?"

"Yes, sir. I've been told his mother-in-law will be making all the necessary arrangements."

"Good. Good. Contact the morgue, then, and see to the transporting of the remains."

"Yes, sir."

Dr. Moran covered the still body with a white bed sheet, shaking his head sadly.

"What a pity," he said.

CHAPTER 45

"How strange," Poe thought.

Standing off to one side of the antiseptic hospital room, he had been able to hear every word that the doctor and nurses had spoken.

He could see all as well—including now viewing his own body, as it lay stretched out on its bed, covered though it was.

But in his current state of being, he was apparently both unseen and unheard by the living. Indeed, one of the departing nurses had seemingly walked right through him on her way out of the room.

Poe had heard of such things as this. *Out-of-body* events, he believed they were called. Clearly, that was what he was now experiencing.

The physical form of himself upon which he gazed longingly was, he sensed, now naught but an empty vessel.

It was his *true* self—his invisible and incorporeal *soul*—that was looking down upon that lifeless body.

Left alone in the room by the exit of his living caregivers, the ghostly Poe began to ponder the ultimate fate of that soul.

Would it, would he, at any moment be sucked away to join all the others who were hopelessly trapped inside Red Death's insidious pool of souls?

Or, even worse...would his many mortal transgressions prove to be enough to condemn his essence to an eternity of fire and pain within the infernal pits of Hell?

"Neither awaits you, darling," a soft and gentle voice said, as if reading his discorporate thoughts.

Poe whirled in surprise to see, standing nearby, his departed Virginia! Only his eyes could see her, for like him she was a spiritual rather than physical being.

Adding to his delight at being once more in her presence was the fact that her spirit did not have the appearance it had affected when last he saw her. She was not gaunt or tortured in mien. She was not dark and angry.

Instead, she looked exactly as Poe remembered her from the time in her life before the unspeakable illness had consumed her. Pretty as a child, maturity had made her beautiful. That is how she appeared now—as she did when the girl she had been crossed the threshold into full womanhood. Her features were as soft and lovely as Poe recalled.

Clearly, hers was a soul now fully at peace.

But something felt wrong.

"Why are you still here?" Poe gasped, afeared that all his efforts on her behalf had come to nothing.

"I thought you were free!"

"I am, Edgar," the wraith replied softly. "Truly so. I've simply been waiting for you—so that I can take you with me to where I am now going." Her eyes lowered and her voice grew even softer.

"If that's what you want."

Poe could scarce believe his ears, though there was no doubt in his mind as to his wife's sincerity.

"It is—more than anything!" he cried out fervently, reaching out and happily discovering that even in this ephemeral form he was able to grasp one of her dainty hands. Even so, uncertainty crept into his mind.

"But, how...why would you want me," he asked of her, "after all that I did?"

"Poor Edgar," she replied solicitously, laying her other spectral hand alongside his equally discorporate cheek.

"When there is true repentance—sins can be forgiven." She smiled rather wistfully.

"And you're willing to grant me that?" an incredulous Poe asked.

For an instant a dark cloud seemed to descend over Virginia's face. "Do you think I'm lying? That this is some sort of trick?"

"Oh, no!" Poe assured her earnestly. "If you had wanted to do so, you had me firmly in your power on that last night. I was resigned to the pool."

"But you still doubt me?" she asked.

Poe stared intently at her for a pregnant moment before responding.

"No. I see nothing false in your countenance." He sighed. "I suppose it simply drives home even more heavily to me my unworthiness."

"What do you mean?"

"When you don't believe you *deserve* forgiveness…it's hard to imagine anyone could truly, freely *grant* you forgiveness."

"Perhaps that's part of my curse," the spirit woman replied. "Despite everything—the anger, the humiliation, the sense of betrayal –

"Still I loved you." She, too, heaved a weary sigh.

"But I can be at peace," she then told Poe, "if I can truly believe that my love is returned." Her ghostly form glided closer to that of Poe.

"You *do* love me, don't you, Edgar?"

"With all my heart, Virginia!" Poe declared fervently. "And for all of time!"

The last the author would ever know of this world came now, as his once and future wife leaned forward and he felt her lips, like feathers, lightly caress his own. Then, both he and she…simply disappeared.

Gone, together, to that place where pain and sorrow are nevermore.

THE END

ABOUT OUR CREATORS

WRITER –

R. A. JONES - is a native of Oklahoma (originally Indian Territory) where he still resides. R. A. has been a freelance writer and editor for the past thirty years.

His credits include newspaper and magazine columns, articles and short stories. He has been a movie reviewer and commentator in newspapers and on radio. He assisted actor Gary Lockwood (Star Trek; 2001: A Space Odyssey) in the writing of Lockwood's autobiography, *2001 Memories: An Actor's Odyssey*. With Michael Vance, R. A. co-wrote the syndicated comic book and comic strip review column *Suspended Animation* for five years.

The readers of *Comic Buyer's Guide* magazine voted him "Favorite Writer About Comics" in 1985, and in 2006 he was inducted into the Oklahoma Cartoonists Collection Hall of Fame. He has scripted more than 100 different issues of various comic book titles in his career. Among the more noteworthy are Wolverine and Captain America for Marvel Comics; *Harlan Ellison's Dream Corridor* for Dark Horse Comics; and Star Trek: Deep Space Nine for Malibu Comics. He also co-wrote, for Image Comics, *Bulletproof Monk*, which served as the basis for the 2003 movie of the same title. His comic book stories, "Cold Hard Facts" and "Three On A Match" which originally appeared in the magazine *Metal Hurlant*, were short films in France.

His novels include *Deathwalker, Global Star* (written with Michael Vance and Mel Fox), *The Equation* (co-written with Michael Vance), *The Steel Ring*, a superhero book based on characters from one of the earliest publishers of comic books, Centaur. He also wrote the Western thriller, *Gun Glory* and its sequel *Comanche Blood*.

INTERIOR ILLUSTRATOR -

CHUCK BORDELL - was born a poor transistor farmer in the rust belt of western Pennsylvania. His childhood was filled with polluted rivers that he fell in love with anyway, the sound of railroad cars crashing together, and dreams of lusty women of dubious reputation. Eventually, he tired of all things iron and decided to trade rust for heavy metals, moving to Missoula, MT in 1987.

Despite a decided lack of tree cover (comparatively speaking) he found Missoula to his liking and, after earning a degree in Archaeology in 1991, decided to stay and continue his quest for the world record two-headed trout. In the meantime, he discovered that he had some skill in telling stories through sequential art and has since worked for numerous comic book publishers, including Malibu Comics, Caliber Comics, Alpha Productions and Silverline Comics. He has produced artwork for Steve Jackson Games and Dungeon Magazine, along with various illustrations for the Neverworld RPG and the Superdeck Superhero Card Game.

His most recent graphic novel is called Lunatic Fringe and recent gaming books include **GURPS: Traveller** and **Earthdawn: Dragons**. "The Ministry of Wolves," a military fantasy, has been published by SynergEbooks.

COVER ARTIST --

ADAM BENET SHAW –Accomplished painter, illustrator, and comics creator, Adam has garnered acclaim across a number of artistic media. After completing studies at the Cleveland Institute of Art in Ohio, the Edinburgh College of Art in Scotland and Watts Atelier in California, Shaw was selected as an emerging American artist to watch by European gallery owners and exhibited in London, England. He has been featured in "New American Painting", selected multiple times for the Arkansas Art Center's Delta Exhibit, and shown at the prestigious "Red Clay Survey" at the Huntsville Museum of Art. His work has also been shown in over 50 group and solo shows in the US and internationally. His figurative paintings are a prominent part of a 140-foot mural entitled "The History of Cotton" at the National Cotton Exchange Museum, St. Jude's Children's Research Hospital, the National Contact Bridge Museum, and a treasured part of private and corporate collections. He has created storyboards for several motion pictures, including Paramount Pictures' film "Black Snake Moan" directed by Craig Brewer, stage design for operas and corporate events, and character illustrations for the gaming industry. His published graphic novel work includes the series "Dead In Memphis", "Bloodstream" for Image Comics, "David: The Illustrated Novel" from Shepherd King Publishing and "Harpe: America's First Serial Killers" from Cave-in-Rock Publishing. He shares his love of art through teaching and workshops at his studio in the Broad Avenue Arts District in Memphis. Recently he has been painting book covers for pulp publishers Pro Se Productions and Airship 27 Productions.

DEATHWALKER

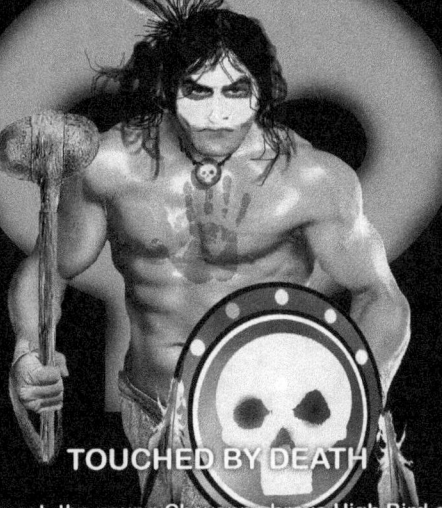

TOUCHED BY DEATH

While on his vision quest, the young Cheyenne brave High Bird encounters the sprit of Death. The powerful wraith recruits the boy as his new agent in the world and High Bird returns to his tribe altered forever as Deathwalker. When the Cheyenne become the target of a vengeful Pawnee Shaman, Stands Alone, only Deathwalker can stand between this evil sorcerer and the total destruction of his people.

Writer R.A. Jones has woven a new and exciting fantasy set against a background authentic Native American lore and culture. He dares to imagine what this wild untamed land would have become had there been no conquests by outside civilizations beyond the great waters. Here is an old world re-envisioned in a bold new action packed adventure worthy of pulp writers such as Robert E. Howard and Edgar Rice Burroughs. Featuring stunning cover art by Laura Givens with interior illustrations by Michael Neno.

Airship27 is proud to present R.A. Jones' DEATHWALKER, another original and quality title in the New Pulp movement.

www.ingramcontent.com/pod-product-compliance
Lightning Source LLC
Chambersburg PA
CBHW051128260626
47170CB00005B/1710